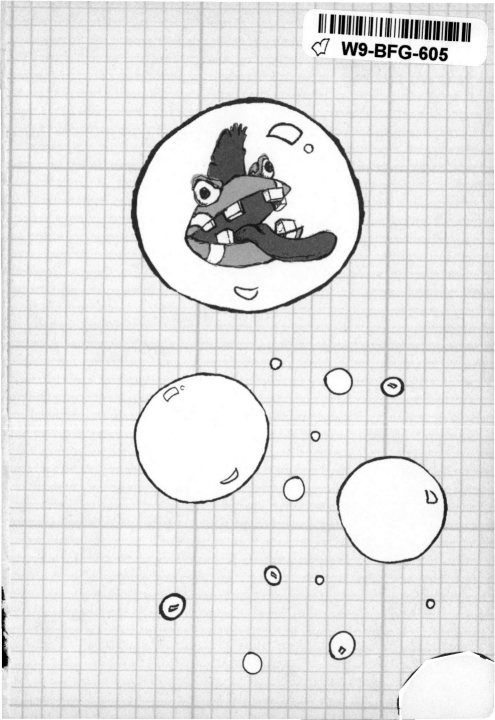

Interior illustrations by
Guy Francis

Little, Brown and Company
Hachette Book Group
237 Park Avenue, New York, NY 10017
Visit our website at www.lb-kids.com

Little, Brown and Company is a division of Hachette Book Group, Inc.
The Little, Brown name and logo are trademarks of Hachette Book Group, Inc.

First Edition: August 2011
Originally published under the title *The Unusual Mind of Vincent Shadow*

ISBN 978-0-316-05666-3

10 9 8 7 6 5 4 3 2 1

RRD-C

Printed in the United States of America

Book design by Saho Fujii

AUTHOR'S NOTE:

Jeff Benz gave out most of the nicknames at Central Middle School. The nicknames were never kind and, unfortunately, they usually stuck. Take Jimmy "Eagle-Eyes" Pierson, for example. Jimmy had an unfortunate eye condition that made it difficult for him to accurately judge distances. Once, in second grade, Jimmy walked into the cafeteria wall so hard it knocked him to the floor. Jeff Benz immediately stood up and yelled, "Nice going, Eagle-Eyes." And that was that. The nickname Eagle-Eyes was now pinned to Jimmy Pierson for the rest of his life. (It didn't matter to anyone that Jimmy had corrective surgery last year and now enjoyed perfect vision. No, to the students at Central Middle, Jimmy Pierson would be "Eagle-Eyes" forever.)

Vincent Shadow didn't have a nickname, but as he climbed out of his secret attic laboratory at 6:34 AM on Monday morning, he was afraid that today would be the day he'd receive one. Vincent was blue. His hands were blue. His face was blue. Even the whites of his eyes were blue. As he closed the hidden door in the back of his bedroom closet, all he could think about were the awful nicknames that Jeff Benz would assign to him.

"Pretty bird. Pretty bird," Nikola said from inside his cage.

"Sshhh. You'll wake everyone up," Vincent said to the African Grey parrot his parents had given him for his ninth birthday. Vincent named the bird after his favorite inventor, Nikola Tesla. And the fact that even his beloved parrot was mocking him was a bad sign of what was to come.

Vincent quietly opened his bedroom door and looked out into the hall. His oldest stepsister, Gwen, usually hogged the bathroom in the morning. But no one was awake yet. So he tiptoed into the bathroom and locked the door.

"Wigman," Vincent said to himself. "The Huli Wigman of New Guinea. That's what they're going to call me. 'Wigboy.'"

Vincent's class had learned about the Huli tribe last year. They got a kick out of hearing that the Huli Wigmen dyed their skin blue for tribal ceremonies. But looking in the mirror, Vincent's worries turned from his new nickname to his own safety. Not only were his skin and eyes blue, but his tongue and teeth were a deep navy blue as well. Vincent had experienced many mishaps in the lab—spills, cuts, little electrical shocks, and once he even glued his fingertips together—but this, this looked much worse.

Vincent stood in the shower for thirty minutes, scrubbing as hard as he could, but nothing seemed to work. He tried all of his sister's fancy soaps and shampoos, but the mess just got worse. Not only was he still as blue as a blue jay, but now most of the bathroom was blue, too.

"Hurry up, Vern," Gwen said as she pounded on the bathroom door. "You've been in there for almost an hour!"

Vincent's father, Norton Shadow, had remarried a few months ago, and Vincent went from being an only child, which he deeply missed, to living with three stepsisters: Gwen, Stella, and Anna. Gwen was sixteen and went to Central High School on the Upper West Side. Stella was Vincent's age. In fact, their birthdays were exactly one week apart. But that was where the similarities stopped. Anna was six. An aggressive, annoying, insistent six-year-old girl.

Gwen had called Vincent "Vern." She had never done this before—called him Vern, that is. She had also never called him Vincent. In fact, she had never called him the same name twice. While the names usually started with a V, she never seemed to come up with "Vincent," or even "Vinny," for that matter. Vincent was pretty sure she did this on purpose. It drove him crazy, but no one else in the family seemed to notice.

"I'LL BE OUT IN A MINUTE," Vincent shouted to Gwen,

who was now practically breaking down the bathroom door with her slipper.

Vincent tried to clean up as best he could and then wrapped a towel around his body, a second around his hair, and covered his face with a third towel as he walked out of the bathroom.

He decided to wear a blue shirt, blue pants, and blue socks to try to camouflage his blueness. Vincent hoped that people would think it was his blue clothes casting a blue reflection that made him seem so blue. But when he looked into his dresser mirror and saw the Wigman chief staring back at him, he realized that this was going to be the longest day of his life.

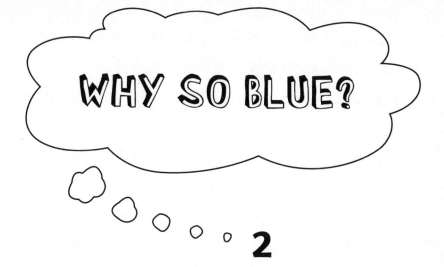

WHY SO BLUE?

2

Anna was sitting at the table eating a bowl of cereal when Vincent walked into the kitchen.

"Mom! Mom! Vincent is *blue*!" obnoxious Anna said. Vincent's stepmother was standing at the sink with her back to Vincent. While the world may be full of wonderful, kind, caring stepmothers, unfortunately for Vincent, Vibs, his new stepmother, was not one of them. Vibs was nice enough to Vincent when Vincent's father was around, but this morning Vincent's dad was in Minneapolis on a job interview, and that meant that Vincent was likely to get the full force of her awfulness.

In fact, Vincent's dad was actually in Minneapolis on his second interview at the Minneapolis Institute of Arts. Vincent was terrified that his dad might get the job. Then they would have to leave New York—and his inventions.

On a normal day, that thought would have occupied his mind, but on this particular blue Monday, Vincent was more afraid of what Vibs would do when she turned around to find the great Huli Wigman chief in her kitchen. But she didn't turn around.

"Why are you blue this morning, Vincent?" she asked.

"I don't know," Vincent answered.

"No, Mom. I mean he *is* blue," Anna insisted.

"We all get a little blue from time to time, Anna. Now be quiet and eat your breakfast," Vibs said.

Gwen walked in and sat down next to Vincent. The noise from her headphones drowned out the awful sound of Anna chomping away on her cereal.

"VANCE, WOULD YOU PLEASE PASS THE MILK?" Gwen said. Vincent passed the milk. Gwen didn't notice he was blue.

Maybe this isn't going to be so bad after all, Vincent thought to himself.

But that thought was interrupted by a scream.

"WHAT DID YOU DO NOW?" Vibs yelled. "Is this some kind of joke? Do you think this is funny? Are you trying to hurt me? IS THAT IT? YOU WANT TO HURT ME? Why do you always have to be so weird?"

Vincent could feel his eyes watering. No matter how hard he tried, he couldn't stop from crying.

"Get upstairs and wash your face," Vibs said as she pointed to the bathroom at the top of the stairs.

"I—" his voice cracked. "I already tried."

"Well, try again!"

Vincent got up and walked out of the kitchen. He passed Stella on the stairs.

"Why so blue?" Stella said with a smile.

Vincent ignored her, walked up the stairs, and slammed his bedroom door behind him.

"What's wrong with Vincent?" Stella asked her mom as she walked into the kitchen.

"I have no idea what's wrong with that boy," Vibs replied.

THE MINI APPLE

3

Vincent's dad, Norton Shadow, had been the assistant director at the Metropolitan Museum of Art for as long as Vincent could remember. Vincent was born in New York City and his parents practically raised him at "the Met." He loved the Met. Or at least he did until his mom died.

Vincent's mother had been an artist. On weekends, she and Vincent would spend hours walking through the Met, looking at all the wonderful paintings. In fact, that's where Vincent learned to draw.

His mother taught him how to recreate works by Picasso, Dalí, Escher, and Hopper. It had been years since anyone had seen Vincent without a black Moleskine notebook. He carried one everywhere he went, but it was toy inventions, not art, that now filled the pages of his notebooks.

Vincent hadn't set foot inside the Met in over two years. Not since his mother died. It wasn't the same without her. And his father wasn't the same without her either.

After his mother's death, Vincent's dad threw himself into his work. So did Vincent. With his dad out of the house, Vincent was able to spend hours in the secret attic lab his mom had helped him build. But all that changed one day when his dad wandered into an online chat room for widowed parents. That is where he met Vibs. They were married shortly thereafter and Vibs and her daughters moved to New York.

Vibs was from Minnesota. Vincent had visited the Mayo Clinic when his mom was sick and remembered Minnesota as painfully cold. He had no interest in ever returning to the Mayo or to Minnesota again. But if his father was offered the job at the Minneapolis Institute of Arts, Vincent knew he would be leaving New York forever.

A WALK IN THE PARK

4

Vincent waited until Vibs had left for work to go downstairs.

"So, what's up with the blue skin?" Stella asked as Vincent walked into the kitchen.

"Don't ask. You wouldn't believe me if I told you."

"All right. Well, come on, little boy blue. We're going to be late for school," Stella said as she lifted her overstuffed backpack.

Even though they were in many of the same classes, Vincent's backpack was much lighter than Stella's. He didn't take school as seriously as she did. It wasn't that he didn't like it; it was just that he'd sometimes think about other things. An entire class could pass without him hearing a single word the teacher said. That never happened to Stella.

As far as stepsisters went, Vincent thought Stella was okay. They weren't exactly best friends, but Stella made him laugh and it was nice to finally have someone to eat lunch with in the cafeteria.

"Oh, wait. Mom left your migraine medicine out for you," Stella said, motioning to the large pill sitting on the kitchen counter.

Mom? Vincent thought to himself. She wasn't his mom. Vincent grabbed a glass out of the cupboard, filled it with water, and carefully pretended to swallow the pill. He cupped the pill in his hand and made a loud gulping sound. He had to do this magic routine every morning, and every morning everyone fell for it.

Vincent and Stella were already late for school. This didn't bother Vincent, but Stella hated to be late for anything.

"Come on, walk faster," she said as they cut through Central Park.

Even though Vincent was in no hurry to see Jeff Benz and find out what horrible nickname awaited him, he was now running to keep up with Stella. And the sight of a small blue boy chasing after a young girl didn't go unnoticed . . . even in New York City.

But just before he could catch up to Stella, Vincent saw streaks of light and everything went blurry. Vincent knew this would be followed quickly by total darkness. He looked around for a park bench—too late. He couldn't see a thing.

"Wait," Vincent yelled to Stella. But she was already out of earshot.

Something was now coming at him out of the darkness. It was small and moving fast. Maybe a football, he thought. As it got closer, Vincent could see it had teeth. No, fangs. Razor-sharp fangs with globs of drool hanging off them. This was no ordinary ball. This ball had fierce red eyes and a piglike snout bent backward.

Its mouth was open wide and it was definitely on the attack. Instinctively, Vincent fell to the ground just as the ball was inches from his face.

This was Vincent Shadow's 49th toy idea. He called it the "Biting Beast Ball." A football with a mouth. Pull the Beast Ball's tongue and its mouth would open to reveal "razor-sharp" foam fangs. Throw the ball just like you would a regular football, but instead of catching the ball, watch it bite onto your opponent's arm.

"Are you okay, Vin?" he heard Stella ask. "Is it a migraine?"

The Beast Ball was floating in front of Vincent. It was the only thing he could see.

"I'm okay. Can you just help me up?"

Stella took Vincent by the hand and led him to a bench near Turtle Pond.

"Are you sure you're not just trying to get out of going to school with blue skin?"

"Wouldn't you?" Vincent said with a smile.

"Your dad said your migraines could be blinding, but I had no—"

"I'm fine," Vincent cut her off. "I just need a few minutes. You go on to school and I'll be right behind you."

"Do you really think I would leave you like this? In Central Park?"

"Hey, I'm a blue kid on a park bench," Vincent said. "That's weird even by New York standards. I'll be fine."

"It's none of my business," Stella's voice softened, "but maybe if you took your migraine medicine you wouldn't have this problem."

"Amazing," Vincent accidentally said out loud as he turned the Beast Ball around in his head.

"I'm just looking out for you."

"No. Yeah, wait—what do you mean, Stella? I

do take my pills. Every morning." He tried to sound convincing.

"Do I look as stupid as the others?"

"I don't know," Vincent said with a smirk on his face. "Remember, I can't see."

"I watch you throw the pills in the sink or slip them in your pocket."

Vincent smiled. "Busted."

"So why don't you take them? Maybe it would help."

Vincent hesitated. "I would take migraine medicine if I had migraines."

Stella stared at him expectantly.

"I would rather not talk about it," Vincent continued. "Please don't tell my dad. He can't know that I had one of my attacks."

"I'm sure he just wants what's best for you, Vincent." Stella now sounded concerned.

Vincent desperately wanted to tell her the truth, but he didn't think she would understand. The visions. The inventions. The lab. All of it. It was a secret he and his mother had kept and he knew it was best if it stayed that way.

"I'll be okay. Can you just take me back home? A little sleep and I'll be good as new."

THE DISCOVERY

5

"Hey, that inventor you like is on the front
page of the newspaper," Stella said as she and Vincent
crossed the street a few blocks from their house.

"Which inventor?" Vincent liked several inventors.
"Nikola Tesla? Thomas Edison? Howard Whiz?"

"The guy you named your bird after."

"Nikola Tesla," Vincent answered. "Wait! Stop walking!" Vincent now desperately wished the Beast Ball

would go away so he could see clearly. "What does the article say?"

"A big headline says 'TESLA ARTIFACTS DISCOVERED' and there's a picture of him," Stella said as she started to pull Vincent forward. "Come on, Vin. I'm already late for first period."

Vincent shook his hand loose from her grip and pulled two dollars out of his pocket. At least he thought it was two dollars, but he couldn't say for sure.

"Here, please buy me a copy. Please, Stella." Vincent held out the money in the general direction he believed Stella was standing. She took the money, bought the paper, and smacked him in the chest with it.

"Thank you," Vincent said. "Now will you read it to me?"

"No." Stella pulled him faster. She got Vincent into the house and up to his room.

"Are you sure you'll be okay if I leave?"

"I'll be fine. I have a little experience with this, Stella."

"Should I call my mom?"

"No. Remember, no one can know about this. Please. When you get to school, just tell the office that I'm out sick today."

Stella reluctantly agreed to keep the entire episode a secret.

Finally alone, Vincent anxiously waited for his sight to return. Vincent's mother had introduced him to Nikola Tesla shortly after his eighth birthday—and shortly after his first toy idea had hit him. He was dying to know what kind of artifacts put Tesla on the front page of the *New York Times*.

EVERLASTING

6

Biting Beast Balls had come to Vincent
the same way his previous ideas had—in a blinding
flash. The ideas always started with flashes of light and
then—bam!—a complete toy would be floating in front
of him. Sky Writerz, Fib Finder Penz, Transplantz, Bubble
Chase—all forty-nine ideas had come to Vincent that
way. The ideas looked so real he often tried to touch
them, only to grab a handful of air.

Vincent could see every hair, every gear, every detail of each invention. But when it hit, the invention was the *only* thing Vincent could see. The rest of the world went black. Sometimes the blindness only lasted a few seconds. Sometimes it would last for hours.

Vincent's first idea hit him three years ago on his eighth birthday. It was the Everlasting H2O Gun, a squirt gun with a built-in dehumidifier so it would never run out of water.

Vincent had been playing catch with his father in the park. His dad had just released the ball when Vincent saw flashes of light, and then his world went black for the first time. The ball hit him in the forehead, knocking him to the ground. Vincent could hear his father's voice, but the only thing he could see was a giant green and gold squirt gun floating in front of him. This terrified him. And when he told his parents, it terrified them, too.

Three more ideas struck Vincent that week. Each

one was accompanied by flashes of light, darkness, and then an incredible toy invention. Vincent quickly realized that he could spin, twist, and even play with the inventions in his head. He was sure he was going crazy. His parents were sure he was sick.

They took him from doctor to doctor. Each one poked, prodded, and took blood. Lots of blood. And asked questions. Lots of questions. But none of the doctors had answers.

The night before Vincent was to visit yet another doctor, his mom stopped in his room to kiss him good night, as she did every night. Vincent was busy sketching in his notebook, as he did every night. But he wasn't sketching Picassos, van Goghs, or Salvador Dalís. He was drawing baseball bats that would quadruple in size when swung, bubble wands that would capture sound in the bubbles, and rockets that would soar high up in the sky and pop into kites. His mom asked him about the sketches, and Vincent said they were his ideas. His inventions.

It was then that Vincent's mom realized her son had a gift. She remembered reading that the great inventor Nikola Tesla had similar blinding experiences as a young man.

But to Vincent the visions were no gift. "Why can't I be like everyone else?" he asked. He knew the kids at school would call him "crazy" if they found out that he saw things. He made his mom promise never to tell anyone about his inventions. Not even his father. She agreed to keep the secret and promised to help him draw and build his toy inventions. From that day on, they would attribute Vincent's blinding spells to migraines.

More than twenty toy ideas hit Vincent in the following six months. His mother helped him with his sketches, and on the nights and weekends that Vincent's dad was working, they built a secret lab—complete with a hidden door—in the unfinished attic space behind his closet. They filled the lab with everything they would need to bring his inventions to life: hammers, saws, drills, test tubes, beakers, glue, duct tape. His mother even created an elaborate alarm system to warn Vincent whenever someone was coming up the stairs. They spent almost ten months working on the secret lab before she got sick.

That was two years ago. Since then, Vincent spent most of his free time in the lab working on his inventions. Just as Tesla had—and just as his mother would have wanted him to do.

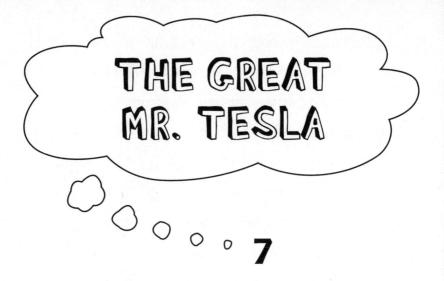

THE GREAT MR. TESLA

7

After a short nap, Vincent opened his eyes and the Biting Beast Ball was gone. He jumped out of bed, looked around his room, and grabbed the *New York Times* Stella had set on his dresser. On the front page, there was a black-and-white photo of a very old Nikola Tesla, with the following story.

TESLA ARTIFACTS DISCOVERED,

NEW YORK—The recent sale of the historic Hotel New Yorker to Ramada Worldwide has unearthed an unusual treasure: Several dozen inventions from the great inventor and former hotel guest, Nikola Tesla, were discovered shortly after the purchase of the historic hotel.

"It is standard procedure to conduct a complete and comprehensive audit of the books," said Colleen Stanton, Executive Vice President of Global Acquisitions for Ramada Worldwide. "But the results of this audit were anything but normal."

Stanton's audit revealed that a payment was made to the Manhattan Storage and Warehouse Company every year since 1943. Upon questioning the staff at the New Yorker, no one could account for the payments. Stanton's investigations led to the discovery of a storage room full of Tesla's notebooks and inventions previously believed to be missing.

"Well, we were all obviously dumbfounded when we opened the door to the storage unit and found the technological remains of one of the greatest inventors of all time. Tesla meant so much to New York, and Ramada is very proud to play a part in his legacy," Stanton added.

In 1935, at the age of 79, Nikola Tesla found himself a resident at the Hotel New Yorker, where he stayed until he died in his sleep on January 7, 1943. The morning after his death,

Tesla's nephew arrived at his uncle's room only to discover that the scientist's body had been removed and his technical papers and prototypes were missing.

It was later reported that representatives from the Office of Alien Property went to the Hotel New Yorker and seized all of Tesla's belongings and transmitted them under seal to the Manhattan Storage and Warehouse Company. In all, two truckloads of papers, furniture, and artifacts were placed under seal.

"The inventions represent an important part of America's past and would make a great addition to any museum's collection," Stanton said. Ramada Hotels plans to auction off the Tesla artifacts next month.

☆✩✩

Vincent lay in his bed thinking about the Tesla inventions. He wondered which prototypes had been discovered and why the government would have seized them in the first place. He looked at the clock and realized his sisters would be home from school soon, and he still needed to clean up his big blue mess.

THE SECRET LAB

8

Vincent went downstairs and grabbed a bucket and a mop from the basement. He took several towels from the upstairs hall closet, paused for a moment, and then reached back in and grabbed Gwen's hair dryer. With his cleaning supplies in hand, Vincent opened the hidden door in the back wall of his bedroom closet and crawled inside.

The lab was surprisingly large, extending back over

thirty feet, but even at four foot six, Vincent was unable to stand up straight in most of the lab. There were several tables in the middle of the lab that served as workbenches. All the table legs had been shortened, allowing Vincent to work on his knees.

Hundreds of sketches covered the walls and ceiling. A stack of black Moleskine notebooks was piled just to the left of the door. Bricks and boards were carefully stacked along the length of the room, creating a long, makeshift bookshelf. The bottom row was mainly books on chemistry, electricity, gravity, Nikola Tesla, and Thomas Edison. The second shelf was lined with old mayonnaise and peanut butter jars containing past failed experiments. Hundreds of failed experiments with handwritten labels: "glow-in-the-dark colored bubbles," "fuzzy paint," "self-drawing ink," "colored fog," and "no-melt snow."

The third shelf held working prototypes. Some of his

favorites included: Bounce 'N' Bubblez, GyroSkatez, B.I.G. Ammo, BlabberBackwardz, RAINbow Rocketz, Soundbreroz, and one of his latest inventions called Mixablez. Mixablez were mixed-up stuffed animals. The prototype was part elephant and part giraffe.

The top shelf held several strange devices that looked like handheld vacuum cleaners and seventy-six jars containing a black liquid. Each jar was dated, labeled with the words "Pop Tunz solution," and identified as a different sound. Sounds like "barking dog," "dad's guitar," "police siren," and "Mom's voice." These were all failed attempts at creating the world's first sound bubbles.

Vincent had successfully created a magnetic bubble solution by adding dishwashing detergent to his self-drawing ink invention. He hoped to build a bubble-blowing device that would allow him to record sound, and even music, into the bubble solution. The device would then create bubbles that carried the sound until they popped and then released the recorded sound for everyone to hear.

Pop Tunz was his mom's favorite invention. They had spent several months working on it. And they had some success. They had trapped a variety of sounds in bubble solutions, including his mother's voice. However, the messages were so faint they were hard to hear. Vincent needed a way to amplify the sound waves. But he hadn't worked on Pop Tunz since his mother had died.

Vincent had been working on Mood Paintz this morning when the experiment exploded in a mess of clear paint that quickly turned blue. He had succeeded in creating a color-changing paint, but instead of changing colors to match the viewer's mood, it matched the mood of the artist. Vincent was sure he could get it to change with the viewer's mood if he could just get the paint solution hotter. Even though heating the solution had caused the explosion in the first place. The hair dryer in the hall closet had given him an idea: Maybe if the paint was stirred rapidly *while* it was heating, it wouldn't explode.

Vincent took a screw-driver from his toolbox and opened the hair dryer. He removed the motor and the fan, which he knew would make an excellent high-speed stirrer, and then placed Gwen's now fanless hair dryer back in the closet.

He spent the rest of the afternoon trying to clean up from the explosion.

SNONKEY THE GREAT

9

Vincent didn't need his lab alarm to tell him Anna was coming; he could hear her bounding up the stairs. He closed the hidden lab door and was crawling out of his closet just as she burst into his bedroom.

"Give 'em back, Vincent!"

"What are you talking about, Anna?"

"Elli and Stretch are missing. I know you took them.

Now give them back!" Anna stamped her feet.

"I have no idea what an elongated stench is and I hope to never find out. Now get out of my room."

"What were you doing in the closet?" Anna asked.

Stella walked into Vincent's room, wondering what all the commotion was about.

"Great. A party in my room. Why don't we invite the rest of New York?" Vincent said.

"Elli and Stretch are missing and I know he took them," Anna said as she stomped, this time on Vincent's foot.

"Ouch!" Vincent yelled, hopping on one foot while holding the other. "I don't know what she's talking about."

"Elli and Stretch are two of her stuffed animals. An elephant and a giraffe," Stella said.

"Oh. Well, I assure you I don't have an elephant or a giraffe," Vincent said. And technically, he was right. He had cut them apart and sewn them together, making one new Mixablez he named Snonkey the Great.

"Why do you blame me for everything?" Vincent asked Anna.

"Because it's always your fault!" Anna said as she stormed out of Vincent's room.

"Here's your homework." Stella set a stack of books on Vincent's desk. "I'm glad to see you're feeling better. And you don't look so blue anymore."

Vincent followed Stella downstairs to the kitchen. Gwen was standing in front of the open refrigerator, just staring in.

"Hi, Gwen," Vincent said, more as an experiment than a greeting.

"Hey, Vic," she said without looking up.

Well, at least she got three letters right. Vincent heard the front door open and ran to see his dad, only to find Vibs. Alone.

"Oh, hi," Vincent said, unable to hide his disappointment. "I thought you were my dad."

"Your father had to go right from the airport to the museum. I guess the Met has been asked to catalog some inventor's artifacts for an auction next month and your father has to work late. Now get washed up. I bought Chinese."

Vincent spent the rest of the night looking through his books about Tesla. He couldn't sleep. He was dying to know what incredible things might have been discovered in Tesla's storage room, and he wondered why his father hadn't called to tell him about it.

DEATH RAYS, PEANUT BUTTER, AND OTHER DANGEROUS THINGS

10

Norton Shadow spread a thick layer of butter on his toast, covered that with peanut butter, and shoved the entire thing into his mouth. This was his breakfast most mornings, and this morning was no exception.

Disgusting. That was the thought of everyone at the

table. Everyone but Vincent. He didn't even notice his dad's inch-thick cholesterol sandwich. He was too busy firing Tesla questions at his father.

"Did you actually see the artifacts? How many were there? Did you touch them? Do they work? Did they find any notebooks? Anything that looked like a death ray? Or an earthquake machine? Were there any pictures?"

"Stawp, stawp." Norton tried to talk but the peanut butter had cemented his mouth shut.

"Im dawnt naw whattwh." Norton stopped and took a sip of his coffee. He swished it around his mouth to melt the peanut-flavored cement.

Vincent couldn't stand the wait. He had stayed up all night reading about the fantastic inventions Tesla was rumored to have been working on while living at the Hotel New Yorker. Death rays that could send beams over 250 miles. Earthquake machines capable of shaking several city blocks. And even a device that could shoot a beam into a person's eye and record his or her thoughts.

"What did you say? I couldn't understand you."

"I said"—Norton had obviously succeeded in swallowing the mass of mush— "I'm not sure what we got. Why don't you stop by after school and see the stuff for yourself."

Vincent was excited about the chance to see the Tesla artifacts, but he didn't like walking inside the Met alone. Without his mother. After all, it had been their place.

"Okay. Maybe."

Stella was shocked to hear the excitement leave Vincent's voice. "I'll go with you," she offered.

"Yeah?"

"Sure," Stella said. "It could be kind of interesting and I always love the Met."

Just then they heard a bloodcurdling scream from upstairs.

"Oh my God, it's Gwen," Vibs yelled as she ran out of the kitchen and up the stairs with the entire family in tow.

Another scream.

"What is it, honey?" Vibs shouted.

They found Gwen standing in the bathroom holding the hair dryer. The entire second floor of the house was thick with the stinging smell of burnt hair. Over-permed, over-produced, burnt high school hair.

"Are you okay?" Norton asked.

"I turned it on and, and—like— the whole thing— like—sparked. I could

have been—like—murdered or something," Gwen said.

She was clearly fine, just a little shocked.

"It's okay. It's okay," Stella said. "Here, just hand me the murder weapon." She took the smoking hair dryer from Gwen's hand.

Vincent could feel Anna glaring at him with those obnoxious little-girl eyes.

"What?"

THE ART OF INVENTION

11

"Hi, Vinny," a woman yelled as Vincent
and Stella entered the Metropolitan Museum of Art.

She was an orange woman who looked to be in her
mid-nineties. She wore an orange skirt and an orange
and black floral shirt, capped off with blaze-orange
hair.

"Hey, Aunt Bonnie." Vincent waved.

"Hi, honey. Well, your father said you were coming in

today and would you look at how much you've grown! It has been so long since we've seen you. We miss you around here and hi, hon, you must be one of Norton's new kids," Bonnie said without taking a breath.

"Hi. I'm Stella."

"Stella, this is my Aunt Bonnie, one of the museum's oldest and dearest volunteers," Vincent said with a smile—the kind of smile you give to a ninety-year-old aunt museum volunteer.

"Well, Vinny, I can't believe how much you've grown—you know I used to babysit Vincent when he was little, and I can't begin to tell you how much we all miss him and—oh hon, we miss your mom so much around here. And boy, I don't have to tell you how much we're going to miss your father. No, no, no," Bonnie said.

"Miss my father?" Vincent asked.

"Well, of course we're going to miss him. Of course

we are. And it gets so cold in Minnesota—you need to make sure and wear a hat and jacket and mittens, too, Vinny," Bonnie said.

"Well, now, come on, your dad said you wanted to see that inventor's stuff and it's all downstairs being unpacked." Bonnie walked toward the elevators. Vincent and Stella followed.

The artifacts were being unpacked, photographed, and cataloged. Dozens of devices had already been tagged and were spread out on two twenty-foot tables in the middle of the room. Vincent walked back and forth along the tables taking it all in. He was shocked at the detail given to the prototypes. Each one looked like a work of art. The wood bases were stained and hand-carved with elaborate moldings. Most of the brass still had its luster. He recognized one of the devices, a device called a Tesla coil. He touched it.

"What do you think this does?" Stella asked.

"Oh, hon, I wouldn't know," Aunt Bonnie said, assuming the question was directed at her.

"It's a Tesla coil. It produces high-frequency alternating currents," Vincent said, having just read about them the night before.

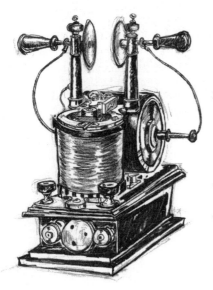

"Oh, oh dear," Aunt Bonnie said.

"What's this?" Stella asked. She was standing in front of a small device with handles attached to two large discs.

"Geez, I have no idea. Wow, look at that!" Vincent pointed

to a device that looked like a small ship engine with metal tubing and gauges sticking out on all sides.

"Look at this wild thing," Stella said, standing in front of a small invention with a series of nine evenly spaced discs. "Do you think it still works?"

"I don't know." It hadn't occurred to Vincent that the inventions might actually still work.

"This thing looks like a crank. Should I try it?" Stella asked.

They both looked at Aunt Bonnie.

"Knock yourself out," she said. "Just don't let anyone see you."

Stella carefully began to turn the crank. Vincent could feel a breeze coming from the device, even though there were no moving parts. Stella turned the crank faster and a spark jumped from one of the middle plates. She let go of the crank and jumped too.

"Oh, careful, hon," Aunt Bonnie said. "Who knows what these things can do."

"Well, is it everything you hoped for?" Norton asked as he entered the room.

"It's pretty cool," Stella said.

"It's amazing!" Vincent was so excited he forgot all about Minnesota. He opened his notebook and started to sketch the device in front of him.

"I just want to sketch a couple of these inventions,"

Vincent said, his pencil already moving quickly over the page.

"Wow, Vincent, I had no idea you could draw like that. That's incredible," Stella said.

"Thanks."

"Just like his mother," Norton said. "Take as much time as you need, Vincent. Come on up to my office when you're done."

Vincent sat on his bedroom floor that night, surrounded by books about Tesla. He had spent hours sketching all the devices at the Met. His hand hurt, and he wished he had thought to bring a camera. But he hoped his sketches would help him figure out which Tesla inventions he had seen. He was sure one of the devices had to be the famous death ray or the earthquake machine.

In one of his books, Vincent managed to find a picture of the invention with the two handles attached to the discs. It was not a death ray, but some sort of high-voltage medical device. He also found a photo of the device with the tubes and the gauges sticking out of it. Unfortunately it was only a steam turbine. Vincent had been sure that it was the earthquake device.

By 3:00 in the morning, Vincent had identified all but one of the inventions from the Met. He could not find anything that looked like the bizarre device Stella had fired up. He looked through a book containing over 300 Tesla patents and found nothing. Why hadn't Tesla patented this one? He had patented all the other inventions in the basement of the Met.

Maybe it wasn't finished? Vincent thought to himself. *Or maybe it was finished and Tesla didn't want anyone to know about it? Maybe it was the death ray!*

LAST CHANCE

13

Vincent was wearing his favorite New
York Yankees jersey with the number "2" and the letters
"SHADOW" stitched on the back. He had his kneepads
and padded vest on for protection. He wore his
catcher's mask with his Yankees hat turned backward.
It had been a long time since he had worn this stuff and
he was surprised it still fit. He reached down into the
box of supplies he had gathered from various rooms

and people in the house: one tube of toothpaste, one electrical cord, a bottle of dishwashing detergent, two bottles of contact lens solution, WD-40, an electric golf ball return with a high-powered electromagnet, twenty-four soft rubber worms, and one Whizzer Mega Doodlez. Check.

Vincent hadn't worked on Pop Tunz in nearly two years, but the scars from his last batch of bubbles were still visible on his hands, and he had a permanent white spot in his hair where a bubble had landed. He knew from experience that the baseball equipment would most likely prove to be no match against the bubbles, but he had to try. Before it was too late.

A few nights after his Met visit, Vincent's dad had finally told him about the job in Minneapolis. And he was quick to point out all the wonderful things the Midwest had to offer and the wonderful new life they would have in Minnesota. Vincent didn't listen. He didn't want a new life. He wanted his old life. But thanks to his father's new job, the moving truck would arrive in the morning.

Vincent had packed up his room. His books. His posters. Even Nikola's bird toys were carefully packed in a box. But he couldn't pack his lab. Pop Tunz had been his biggest disappointment. He had always planned to work on it again. He thought he had time. But now he was out of time. This was it. His last night in the lab. He needed to focus. He also needed a lot of luck.

Vincent pulled the old sheet off his bubble still, and dust filled the air. He went straight to work. He took a handful of the rubber worms he had borrowed from his dad's tackle box and began melting them in a pot. Then he mixed in a half cup of detergent and a dab of toothpaste. Next he cut open Anna's Mega Doodlez and dumped the metal shavings into an old coffee can. He poured in two bottles of contact lens solution. Vincent knew from experience that the salt in the contact lens solution would speed the rusting process. He placed the coffee can under the blender and turned it on.

Vincent let the blender run and started to work on the Pop Tunz bubble-blowing device. He grabbed one of the large bubble-blower prototypes off the top shelf and removed the battery panel. He took out the six D batteries. He needed more voltage than Gwen's portable stereo batteries could provide. So he decided to test the bubble blower using 110 Tesla-invented volts right out of the wall.

He pulled out the electrical cord he had borrowed from the Shadow family DVD player and wired it into the bubble blower. Then he cut open his father's golf putt return and removed the powerful electromagnet. He duct-taped the electromagnet to the bottom of Vibs's large metal mixing bowl.

Vincent turned off the blender and poured the rust-colored liquid into the mixing bowl. He plugged in the electromagnet, and the rusty liquid clung to the sides of the bowl. He unplugged the electromagnet, and the metallic liquid let go of the side of the bowl and ran to the bottom. He poured the liquid from the bowl into a tall glass bottle, boiled the solution until it turned black, and then poured it into a clean glass jar.

He looked at the clock on the wall: 6:30 AM. He would have to move quicker. The movers would arrive soon.

Vincent reached into a drawer and pulled out a large metal loop he had fashioned out of a kitchen utensil. He rubbed the metal loop with sandpaper to remove the rust buildup and then placed it in the bubble-blowing device. He screwed the glass jar with the black liquid onto the bottom of the device.

Vincent pushed down on the red button and said "testing, testing" into the microphone mounted near the back of the bubble blower.

He switched on the device and it made a dull hum. He smiled. That was the sound he had hoped for. He pulled the trigger on the blower and the liquid started to twist and turn inside the glass jar. Vincent clenched his teeth, hoped for the best, and released the trigger.

The liquid leaped from the jar and disappeared up inside the bubble blower. He held the blower high into the air. Dozens of two-inch solid black bubbles started to fill the room. They floated silently through the air. The first bubble to hit the floor was a perfect two-inch bubble. By Vincent's calculations, that should have been large enough to replay his message, but all he heard was the crackle of electricity. Although it was louder than any bubble he had made previously, Vincent was disappointed. He had hoped the increased voltage would amplify the sound waves enough to deliver an audible message. He would need even more volts.

The bubble blower began to glow blue as more than a dozen bubbles hit the floor in what sounded like a nest of angry rattlesnakes. The side of the blower sparked, exploded, and sprayed electrified bubble solution in every direction. Vincent dropped the blower and tucked himself into the fetal position.

Liquid lightning shot up and created a blast that left a large burn mark on the ceiling. A stream of electric bubble solution hit one of the sketches taped to the wall. The sketch burst into flames. Vincent stood up to grab the fire extinguisher as another row of sketches quickly went up in flames. He managed to avoid the electrified bubbles as he pointed the extinguisher toward the fire and pulled the trigger.

THE WHIZ KID

14

"One hundred, one hundred, do I hear one hundred? One, one, one, great. One hundred thousand dollars to the man in back of the room. Two hundred, two, two, two, do I hear two? Two, two, two hundred thousand to the tall man in the white suit. Three, three, can we get three hundred? Three, three, three hundred thousand once again to the man in the back. Five, five, five, five—come on—five hundred thousand. Five, five,

five, five hundred thousand to own a piece of history. Five hundred. Five hundred. Come on, people, Tesla is one of the greatest inventors of all time. Let's go. Five, five, five hundred thousand to the man in white. Six, six, now do I hear six hundred . . ."

Howard G. Whiz had worn a white suit every day for the last sixty-one years. He had an entire closet full of white shirts, white jackets, white pants, white belts, white socks, white shoes, and white ties. But his ties didn't stay white. Every morning at precisely 5:30 AM, he put on a pot of coffee and painted a white tie to wear that day. He painted the tie to match his mood. He painted a new tie every day and never wore the same tie twice.

Each night he would nail that day's tie to the wall in his mansion. This was Howard G. Whiz's diary, and he had done this every day for the last 22,297 days. Today, Howard G. Whiz's tie had a single gold lightning bolt painted on it.

"One, one, one, do I hear one million. One million, one million, one, one, one," the auctioneer said. "Come on, people. Look at the condition of these artifacts. Untouched by human eyes until just last month. One, one, one, can I get one, one, one..."

A rather large man in the front row raised his hand and was immediately jabbed in the ribs by his wife's elbow.

"Well, honey, they have been untouched by human eyes for centuries," he explained.

"Great, one million from the fat man in the front row. Do I hear two, two, two million. Looking for two, two, two, two, who will go two, all right. Two million from the man with the giant scar in the second row. Three, three, three, who's gonna give me three? Three, three. People, we are looking for three, and three million dollars from the man in back. Four, four, four, do I hear four million? Who wants to own a slice of history? Four, four, four, four, where are the Tesla lovers? We need four, four, four, for all these wonderful inventions. Terrific, Colonel Sanders is willing to pay four million dollars. Now who will give me five, five, five . . ."

Much to his father's regret, Howard G. Whiz's parents knew that Howard was unusual almost at birth. At the tender age of three, Howard weaned himself off his pacifier by biting an eighth of an inch off the tip of the pacifier each morning for two weeks. By the end of the second week, his pacifier was gone and so was his desire for one.

"Five million, five million, do I hear five million? Five

million to the man with the scar. Six, six, will anyone go six?" the auctioneer asked.

"Say here." Howard stood up. "Ten million, good boy. I will give you ten million dollars for Mr. Tesla's fine inventions."

Howard G. Whiz could bid ten times that amount if he wanted to, and everyone in the room knew it. Howard had been famous his entire life, thanks mostly to an invention he created when he was just seven years old.

In 1922, Thomas Fairbairn invented an artificial grass from a concoction of cottonseed hulls, sand, oil, and dye. This invention fueled the development of a new game called miniature golf. By 1935, America had become obsessed with miniature golf. And so had Howard G. Whiz's father, Gordon Whiz. Gordon spent hours practicing miniature golf in his living room by putting a golf ball into a coffee can. Gordon made his son Howard sit next to the can, rolling the balls back to him all day.

Obsessed with the new science of electricity and tired of rolling the balls back to his father, Howard decided to invent a device that would automatically return the golf balls. He decided to turn the coffee can into an electromagnet.

When the golf ball entered the coffee can, it would trigger a switch that would run electricity through the wires Howard had wrapped around the outside of the can. The entire coffee can would become an electromagnet, attracting the hammer Howard had mounted to the back of the can. The hammer would swing forward, knocking the ball out of the can and back to his father. It was Howard's first invention and he thought his father would love it. But Gordon was irritated at his son's elaborate attempt to get out of work.

Gordon's irritation quickly turned to glee when visitors started inquiring about buying a coffee can putt return for themselves. Gordon seized the opportunity to make money and forced Howard to spend his days in the cellar building coffee can putt returns. Soon, young Howard was spending fourteen hours a day building the putting devices. He now hated his invention and hated his father for making him build it.

In an effort to have a little fun, Howard nailed several of the electromagnetic coffee cans to a large board. He tilted the board and would roll a golf ball up the board and watch it bounce and shoot from one can to the next as it rolled down. He did this for hours at a time until his father took the board away and told him to focus on his work.

Soon however, Howard's father became fascinated with the board too. Howard's father was sure others would also find the board fascinating, and he sold it to the Bally Manufacturing Corporation a month later. Bally built tens of thousands of the boards over the next fifty years. They called it pinball.

On his eighteenth birthday Howard G. Whiz moved out of his parents' house and never spoke to his father again. Robbed of his youth and weary of the greed that had surrounded him, Howard started the Whizzer Toy Company and vowed never to invent an adult product again. And he never did.

Howard was famous for giving young inventors the support he never received. He held an annual toy contest and always encouraged young inventors to follow their dreams and invent their futures.

"Going once, going twice—sold to the lightning bolt gentleman for a cool ten million dollars. Enjoy your new inventions, sir," the auctioneer said.

"I shall," Howard G. Whiz replied.

FOUR MONTHS LATER

15

Maybe it was because Vincent was the
only boy. Or maybe it was because his bird, Nikola,
made too much noise. Or maybe
it was simply because Vibs was
evil. Whatever the reason, when
the Shadow family moved into
their new house in Minnesota,

Vibs decided Vincent should sleep in the basement "bedroom," which actually wasn't a bedroom at all. It was more of a closet. A small closet with no door. A small closet with no door, a concrete floor, and the world's oldest and loudest washer and dryer located just a few feet away.

And maybe it was the cold Midwestern climate or perhaps the noise from the washer and dryer, or just the simple fact that Vibs was evil, but whatever the reason, Vincent hadn't had a single toy idea since they arrived in Minnesota four months earlier. No flashes of light. No blindness. Not a single idea. And that was okay with Vincent.

He was leaving his failed attempts at inventing behind. He had decided that the move to Minnesota was a chance to start over. No more silly dreams of becoming a great inventor. He left his notebooks, tools, and inventions hidden away in his secret lab forever. He had failed as a toy inventor, but at least no one would ever know.

Vincent, Gwen, Stella, and Anna all attended the Minneapolis School of Art and Design now. MSAD was a small K–12 school connected to the Minneapolis Institute of Arts. The students took a few traditional classes, but most of the focus was on art. A typical day might start with Oil Painting, followed by Ceramics, Metal Sculpture, lunch, Math, Art Ideas, and then a Graphic Design class at the end of the day. In fact, that was Vincent's schedule. And he liked all of his classes. All of them except Math. He loved Art Ideas the most. Mr. Dennis taught Art Ideas and Mr. Dennis was crazy.

FOOBEEZOOBEE

16

"Come on, come on, find a seat, everybody. We have a lot to talk about today," Mr. Dennis said, standing on top of his desk.

No one seemed surprised to see Mr. Dennis standing on his desk. No one would have been surprised to walk into the room and see Mr. Dennis hanging upside down from the ceiling wearing a space suit. Mr. Dennis was crazy and Vincent liked it that way.

"Mike, Gary, John, let's go. Find a seat."

"What are we doin' today, Mr. D? Painting our faces? Acting out art? Throwing things off the roof again?" Gary asked.

"Ooh! Ooh! Can I throw Gary off the roof, Mr. Dennis?" Lori asked.

"No. No. No. We aren't throwing anything off the roof. The folks in the office weren't too happy about that. They failed to see the art. But not to worry, today is far more exciting. Quick, quick, take a seat," Mr. Dennis said, jumping up and down on his desk.

"Good. First, the homework," Mr. Dennis said. "Did everyone bring their sculptures? Good. Good. Please stand up, class, and bring them forward."

There were eight kids left in Mr. Dennis's Art Ideas class. They had started with thirty-two, but most of the kids had switched classes. Not everyone understood Mr. Dennis the way Vincent did.

Vincent pulled out his sculpture. He had worked hard on it for several weeks. Harder than he had ever worked on a school project. It was a field of strange-looking snowdrifts made out of glass. It reminded Vincent of one of his mother's favorite prints at the Met, *The Great Wave off Kanagawa*. Vincent stood at the end of the line, holding his sculpture. And, as usual, Eleanor was at the front of the line.

"Excellent, Eleanor. Please place it in the bin," Mr. Dennis said as he pointed to a large garbage can in front of his desk.

"In here?" Eleanor asked as she pointed at the garbage can.

"Yes. Next, please. Oh my, Ariel. That is beautiful. Did you oxidize the copper yourself?"

"Yeah, it took six days of heating it in the oven and basting it with water every twenty minutes," Ariel said.

"Wonderful, simply wonderful. Please carefully place it in the bin. Next. Very nice, Mike. Please place your art in the bin. Oh wow, Lori. Did you hand-paint all those beads? Wonderful. Please place it in the bin. Careful now," Mr. Dennis said as Lori carefully set her sculpture on top of Mike's in the garbage can.

"Well done, Chris. Please place it in the bin. Brilliant, Gary! Just brilliant. What is it?" Mr. Dennis asked.

"It's like, ah, like a bunch of basketball dudes doing kind of, like, a ballet thing," Gary said.

"In the bin, please," Mr. Dennis said to Gary.

"Oh, John. Well done, you! Is that Paul Klee's *Sunset* recreated in metal mesh? Brilliant! Absolutely brilliant. In the bin, please. Carefully, John."

"Well, well, well, Mr. Shadow. You have outdone yourself this time. Fantastic. Just fantastic. Is that glass?" Mr. Dennis asked.

"Yes. Hand-painted," Vincent answered.

"Oh, oh, no. Well, in the bin. Careful now, Mr. Shadow."

Vincent carefully balanced his glass sculpture on top of the pile of sculptures. He turned to walk back to his desk, but before he could reach it he heard Mr. Dennis yell—

"FOOBEEZOOBEE!"

Vincent turned to see Mr. Dennis standing waist-deep in the garbage can of broken art. The class was speechless. Ariel and Chris burst into tears.

Mr. Dennis crawled out of the garbage can. He pulled two large pieces of broken glass from his leg. He was bleeding.

"Didn't you like the sculptures, Mr. D?" Gary asked.

"They were wonderful. Simply wonderful," Mr. Dennis said.

Trying to fight back his tears, Chris said, "It took me a whole week to finish that. Why did you break it?"

"It wasn't finished, Chris. Art is never finished. It is a process. A journey. Your sculpture was beautiful, but it wasn't finished. It can't be finished. Class, class, please listen carefully. I gave each of you the exact same assignment, and you each came back with very different solutions. Right? And they were all great. They were all perfect."

"Then why did you break them, Mr. D?" Gary asked.

"I wanted to teach you a lesson. An important, albeit hard, lesson."

"What lesson is that?" Chris asked. He was clearly getting more upset by the second.

"There is always more than one right answer," Vincent chimed in.

"Right. Right, Mr. Shadow. Exactly right. There are lots of right answers. And lots of wrong answers. But it is important—it is imperative that when the muse touches you and you feel you have found the answer, you mustn't fall in love with it.

"There are lots of right answers. And if you fall in love with the one you have, you will close your eyes to all the other possible answers. These sculptures were absolutely wonderful. Perfect. Brilliant. All of them. Now, we will do the same assignment again and I want each and every one of you to come back tomorrow with another right answer."

THE CONTEST

17

Vincent stayed up most of the night bending, twisting, and turning a stack of wire clothes hangers into his new sculpture. He was tired and his fingers hurt, but he liked the sculpture. He set it on the kitchen counter and grabbed a bowl from the cupboard.

"What's up with the wiry thing?" Anna asked.

"It's homework," Vincent said as he poured himself a bowl of Cookie Crisp cereal.

"What's it supposed to be?"

"Art," Vincent said.

"It's kind of ugly for art," Anna said as she chomped on her cereal.

"Is that for Mr. Dennis's class?" Vibs asked.

"Yep," Vincent said.

"I thought your sculpture was due yesterday," Vibs said. "What happened to that glass thing?"

"It broke," Vincent said without looking up from his bowl. He knew it was pointless to try and explain Mr. Dennis to Vibs. He finished his cereal and walked to school with Stella. The house his parents had rented was in the heart of Minneapolis, one block from their new school.

Mr. Dennis was a blur as he flew into the room on a brand new cherry-red Whizzer Board 4000. He kicked the jump pedal and soared high into the air, clearing his desk by seven or eight inches. He landed on his feet and stomped one foot down onto the rear flip bar; the board flipped through the air and he caught it with one hand. The class erupted in applause that could be heard all the way down to Mrs. Schmidt's office.

"Thank you, thank you. It was nothing, really. Just a little good, old-fashioned footwork."

"That's the Whizzer Board 4000!" Gary yelled. "Where did you get it?"

"Why, yes, Gary, this is indeed the Whizzer Board 4000. The radical new board from Whizzer Toys. She is a lot to handle. Fast as a panther," Mr. Dennis said. "Do you like it?"

"Yeah, but they're impossible to get. Where did you get it, Mr. D?"

"My cousin sent it to me," Mr. Dennis said as he handed the Whizzer Board 4000 to Gary.

"Who's your cousin?" Vincent asked.

"Well, I'm glad you asked. But first, where is Chris? He missed my big entrance. Should I do it again when he gets here?"

"No need, Mr. D. Chris switched classes," Gary said as he stroked the skateboard.

"Ah, and then there were seven. Shame, shame, what a shame. Well then, Mr. Shadow, the answer to your question is Howie," Mr. Dennis said as he started to write on the whiteboard.

"Oh?" Vincent had no idea what Mr. Dennis was talking about, but then he rarely knew exactly what Mr. Dennis was talking about.

"Oh, you kids probably know him better as Howard G. Whiz, the master toymaker."

"HOWARD G. WHIZ IS YOUR COUSIN?" Vincent shouted.

"Yes," Mr. Dennis said as he finished writing the words "Annual Whizzer Toy Contest" on the board.

"Do you know him?" Lori asked.

"Do you know your cousins?" Mr. Dennis asked her.

"Yeah. Well, not the ones that live out in Washington. But I know my other cousins," Lori said.

"Right, right. Well I do know Howie, I mean Howard, and every year he has a toy contest. And every year I have my students enter the contest," Mr. Dennis said.

"Do the kids ever win?" Gary asked.

"No. No. I've never had a student win, but I've never had a class this large before. So, maybe this is the year. Maybe, just maybe. But, dear Gary, it isn't really about winning and it really isn't about the toys, the inventions, or the trip to New York. It's—"

"Trip to New York, Mr. D?" Gary interrupted.

"Yes, yes, didn't I mention that? Students from all over the world enter the contest. Howie looks through all the invention ideas and selects a handful of kids to build their inventions and bring them to the big Toy Fair in New York. There the kids get a chance to demonstrate their inventions on stage, and the winner is selected."

"What does the winner get?" Gary asked.

"A million dollars?" John shouted.

Mr. Dennis grabbed the Whizzer Board 4000 from Gary's hands and held it above his head. He pushed down on the turbo pedal and the board let out a hefty grunt as the wheels spun furiously. "This, my friends, was invented by a kid just like you, sitting in a classroom just like this. The winner gets to spend the summer at Whizzer Toys inventing toys with my cousin Mr. Howard G. Whiz."

IDEA NO. 50

18

Vincent lay in bed with a pillow over his head. Gwen was doing a late night load of laundry and Vincent knew he wouldn't be able to sleep until the spin cycle was complete.

He was devastated. He had spent his entire life trying to be a toy inventor. Now he had a chance to get his inventions in front of one of his favorite inventors and he had no ideas. He had no idea where his ideas even came from, but he wished one would come to him now. He also wished he hadn't left his notebooks sealed away in his lab.

Vincent remembered reading all about Mr. Whiz buying the Tesla artifacts. Clearly, anyone willing to pay ten million dollars for the Tesla inventions had to be a big Tesla fan. Maybe if Vincent invented a Tesla-like toy it would get Mr. Whiz's attention. Tesla had invented the world's first remote-controlled toy. Maybe Vincent could create a new type of remote-controlled toy.

Vincent sat up and stared at the poster of Nikola Tesla hanging on his bedroom wall. Tesla was standing in a large room with a huge two-story Tesla coil that was throwing bolts of lightning all around the room. Tesla was surrounded by the lightning. Vincent could see from Tesla's hair that the electric discharge from the large coil was creating a lot of wind. Vincent thought

SUGAR AND SPICE, YEAH RIGHT

19

Vincent submitted his windless kite idea and Mr. Dennis loved it. So Vincent went to work collecting the parts he would need for a prototype just in case he was selected to go to the Toy Fair.

He needed a wire no thicker than a human hair and he knew just where to find it. But first he would have to get past Anna.

Vincent got down on his knees and peeked around the corner. Anna was watching TV in the living room. He crawled on his belly behind the couch, but he needed to get to the stairs and there was a five-foot gap between the end of the couch and the stairway. Anna would see him if she turned around. They both knew he had no business upstairs. His "bedroom" was in the basement. In the laundry room.

Vincent moved slowly. He held his breath as he inched along. He made it to the stairs without Anna noticing him. She was engrossed in some annoying little six-year-old-girl show.

Vincent slid the guitar case out from under his dad's bed. He needed a thin wire for his invention and the top E string on his dad's electric guitar fit the bill perfectly. Vincent removed the wire, put it in his pocket, and slid the guitar back under the bed.

"What are you doing?" Anna asked.

"Nothing. I dropped something and was just looking for it."

"You shouldn't be in my mom's room. I know you're up to something, Vincent. And I'm going to tell my mom when she gets home."

Vincent put his hand in his pocket to protect the guitar string.

"Why don't you tell her how annoying you are?" Vincent walked downstairs to his room.

Anna followed.

"Go away, Anna. Leave me alone."

Anna hopped on top of the dryer and just stared at him. He hated having a little sister.

Vincent's kite started to take shape over the next few weeks. He found a diamond-shaped canvas at school and decided to use it as the frame for his kite. He removed the canvas and replaced it with aluminum foil. The shiny metal kite looked like a toy from the future, even if it didn't fly yet.

Vincent borrowed speaker wire from the Shadow family stereo. He tied a three-foot piece of string to the end of the speaker wire and tied the other end of the string to the kite. He wrapped the electric guitar string around the kite string and attached one end to the speaker wire.

He would send high voltage up the speaker wire

to the electric guitar string. When enough electricity built up in the guitar string, it would leap the six-inch gap to the metal kite. The leaping ions would cause an ionic breeze, and the kite would soar into the air. Now all Vincent needed was a way to produce the required high voltage.

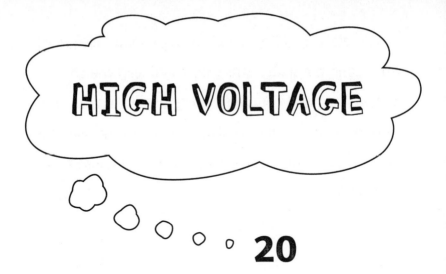

HIGH VOLTAGE

20

Vincent looked into the brown paper bag.

Great, he thought, *a tuna sandwich again.* He hated tuna sandwiches. Particularly the crispy brown tuna sandwiches Vibs put in his lunch every day.

He dumped his lunch onto the cafeteria table. One soft brown banana, a baggie full of corn nuts, and one brown tuna sandwich. Great. Just great.

Vincent looked over at Stella's lunch. One Thermos of piping hot chicken noodle soup. Four saltine crackers. A shiny red apple. One king-size bag of nacho-flavored Doritos. A homemade double-fudge brownie that had been wrapped tightly in tin foil and two scoops of Ben & Jerry's vanilla ice cream packed in a second Thermos to go with the brownie.

"Your mom hates me," Vincent said.

"Do you want my soup?" Stella asked.

"I'll take the brownie."

Stella slid the brownie and ice cream across the table. It was so warm that some of the fudge chunks had melted and formed a pool of molten chocolaty goodness on the tinfoil. Vincent was trying to figure out the best way to eat it when he heard a commotion out in the hall.

"Vincent! Vincent! Vincent Shadow!"

Now the students at MSAD had come to expect the unexpected from Mr. Dennis, and it wasn't unusual for Mr. Dennis to get so excited that he would shake uncontrollably or be unable to catch his breath. But today, Mr. Dennis had taken his excitability to a whole new level.

"Vincent! Has anyone seen Vincent Shadow?"

"IN HERE, MR. D!" Vincent shouted.

Paul Bard dove out of the way, narrowly avoiding a high-speed crash as Mr. Dennis came flying into the lunchroom on his Whizzer Board 4000.

"Vincent! Vincent! Vincent Shadow!" Mr. Dennis yelled.

Vincent stood up, waved his hands in the air and yelled, "OVER HERE, MR. D!"

Now, the Whizzer Board 4000 was a fine machine, representing the latest technology in electric in-line skateboards, but Howard G. Whiz did not have his

220-pound cousin in mind when he designed the brakes for it. But Mr. Dennis did have his cousin in mind as he crashed and slid down twelve feet of table, coming to a stop right atop Vincent's hot fudge brownie. (Unfortunately for Vincent, his crispy brown tuna sandwich was unharmed in the accident.)

"Are you okay, Mr. D?" Vincent asked as a crowd gathered around.

"I'm great, Vincent! Just great. You did it! By golly, you did it!" Mr. Dennis said as he climbed off the table, licking the hot fudge from his face.

"Did what Mr. D?" Vincent asked.

"You did it, Vincent! You did it! You have been selected to demonstrate your windless kite in New York City!"

"Really?"

"Yes, Vincent. Really!" Mr. Dennis reached into his pocket and pulled out fragments of Wonder Bread and part of a Fruit Roll-Up he had collected while sliding down the cafeteria table. He reached back into his pocket and pulled out a piece of paper.

"Here it is, Vincent. You've been invited to demonstrate your windless kite at the Toy Fair next week in New York City. 'One lucky inventor will be selected to work at the Whizzer Toy Company this summer,'" he read, "'turning his or her toy invention into a real Whizzer Toy product.' You're going to New York, Mr. Shadow," Mr. Dennis said as he started to jump up and down. "You're going to New York!"

"What's wrong, Vincent?" Stella asked. "You don't look excited."

"It's the kite. I don't have it working yet."

"I'll help you, Vincent. Don't worry, we'll get it done in time," Stella said.

"Vincent, Vincent, Vincent. There are lots of right answers and we have a week to find one of them," Mr. Dennis said.

"I have the answer. High voltage. That's the answer. I have the kite built, I just need high voltage."

"HIGH VOLTAGE. HIGH VOLTAGE. Well, it's easy to find high voltage. The world is full of high voltage: lightning bolts, power lines, hot tubs, and neon signs. It's easy to find high voltage. They label it for you, Vincent, they label it for you," Mr. Dennis said.

"What do you mean, 'they label it for you'?" Vincent asked.

"Look." Mr. Dennis pulled a TV off the wall. "See this symbol, the lightning bolt in the middle of the triangle?" Mr. Dennis asked.

"Yeah," Vincent said.

"High voltage. They label it for you. Televisions, computer monitors, all have transformers inside them that make—high voltage."

MAYBE NEXT TIME

21

"I'm sorry, Vincent, but there's no way we're letting you go to New York City alone," Vibs said.

Vincent looked to his father. "Please, Dad. Can't you just take a few days off of work and come with me?"

"No, buddy. I'm proud of you, but I'm afraid I agree with Vibs. I'm launching a new Native American exhibit next weekend. I have to be here. I'm sorry, but you're gonna have to sit this one out."

"Please, Dad! This is a really, really big deal. Only six kids from all over the world were selected to go. I really want to go, Dad."

"Maybe next time," Vibs said.

Vincent needed his mother. She would understand how much this meant to him.

"I have worked too hard for too many years to get this close to my dream and just let it go."

"Vincent, you've only been working on that kite for two weeks," Vibs said. "There will be other contests and other trips to New York."

"I could go with him," Stella offered.

"That's sweet, Stella, but—"

"No, really. I would like to go. We could stay with Vincent's Aunt Bonnie." Stella shot Vincent a look that said, "Let me handle this," and Vincent sat back down on the couch.

"Well, I hadn't thought of Aunt Bonnie," Norton said.

"What about school?" Vibs asked.

"The registration dinner is Saturday night and the Toy Fair is Sunday," Vincent said.

"We could fly out Saturday morning and fly back Sunday night," Stella added.

"Well, I guess it would be okay with me if it's okay with Aunt Bonnie," Norton said.

Vincent's eyes widened. He jumped up and hugged his dad.

"Thanks, Dad," Vincent said.

"We'd better get on the computer and check airfares," Vincent's dad said.

"Oh, Norton, honey. You'll have to call the airline on the phone. The computer monitor isn't working."

"First the DVD player and now this! What's next?"

22

Eleven-year-old George Spinowski Jr.
was thrilled to learn his toy invention had been accepted into the annual Whizzer Toy contest. But perhaps no one was more excited by this fact than his father, George Spinowski Sr. To George Sr., the contest was an opportunity for revenge. Revenge that—in his mind—dated back to 1935.

That summer, Nikola Tesla was in the newspapers

recounting his experiments with his earthquake device and death ray machines, and Parker Brothers released the board game Monopoly. But the invention that changed everything for the Spinowski family could be found in the bathroom. That is where you would have found Northern's all new "splinter-free" toilet paper.

On the morning of August 16, 1935, Carl Spinowski walked into the bicycle factory he ran with his brother Mike—George Sr.'s father—with a roll of Northern's new splinter-free toilet paper. Mike, a lifelong practical joker, was preparing yet another one of his pranks involving  itch powder when some of the powder accidentally spilled on the roll of toilet paper. That fortuitous accident forever changed the lives of generations of Spinowskis.

Mike Spinowski instantly realized that itchy toilet paper, sold as a gag gift, could provide the country with the humor it so desperately needed. So in the fall of 1935, the Spinowski Brothers Bicycle Company became the Spinowski Toy and Novelty Company. And by the end of 1939, the brothers were selling fifteen million rolls of novelty toilet paper in sixteen different countries.

Mike died in 1962, leaving the Spinowski Toy and Novelty Company, which was no longer very successful, to his son, George. George Spinowski was a mean, cruel, vicious man, and running his father's toy company was the last thing he wanted to do. But the family was so far in debt that he had no choice. George knew he would have to invent some new toys—and he would have to do it fast.

George thought about his favorite toys growing up, but the truth was that George hadn't really liked toys and didn't really care much for fun. He did, however, have fond memories of his childhood BB gun, which he used to torment the neighbors.

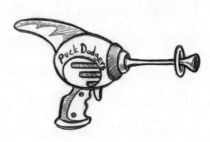

That fall, Spinowski Toys launched the Puck Dodger BB Blaster. It was a high-powered, large caliber BB gun that looked like the gun Puck Dodger used each week on his popular TV show. Kids loved Puck Dodger and they loved the Puck Dodger BB Blaster.

The Spinowski Toy Company enjoyed great success for nearly three decades until the spring of 2002, when Whizzer Toys launched the Whizzer Mega Fizzer and sales of the BB Blaster went in the toilet. George Spinowski vowed he would have his revenge on Howard Whiz and the Whizzer Toy Company.

George was not a lover of science, but the words "Death Ray" in the newspaper headline caught his eye. And when George Spinowski read about the upcoming auction of the recently discovered Tesla artifacts, which were rumored to include a death ray device and an earthquake-generating machine, he was sure his problems were solved. He simply had to outbid the next fellow, and he would have his next big product.

Surely kids would find an actual death ray much more fun than a Whizzer Mega Fizzer. But George hadn't counted on having to outbid Mr. Howard G. Whiz himself. And when Howard raised the bid to ten million dollars, George decided he would have to come up with "plan B."

George Sr. found plan B in the newspaper headlines several weeks later, when he read, "Whizzer Toys to Hold Annual Toy Invention Contest."

STRANGE FLIGHT

23

"Code sixteen. Code sixteen," the airport security guard yelled as he grabbed Vincent's shirt with one hand and Vincent's duffel bag with the other. Five or six security guards immediately surrounded Vincent.

"Please step over here, sir," one of the guards said.

Sir? Vincent thought. *I must be in big trouble if they're calling me "sir."*

"What's wrong?" Vincent asked.

"Please step over here, sir," the man said again. He pushed Vincent down in a chair and carefully placed his duffel bag on a stainless steel table. Now there were over a dozen airport security guards gathered around Vincent's bag whispering to each other.

"Excuse me, miss, are you with the boy?" the man asked Stella, who was still standing in line waiting to go through the metal detector.

"Yes," Stella said. Stella didn't need to ask what the fuss was about. She knew.

"Please step to the side, miss."

Stella took a seat next to Vincent. A crowd of people had gathered, and they were all staring at Vincent and Stella.

One of the guards stepped forward and asked Vincent what was in his bag.

"Oh." Vincent realized that his homemade invention might have looked suspiciously like a bomb when it was x-rayed.

"It's just a kite," Vincent said as he stood up. Two large guards quickly shoved Vincent back in his chair.

"No, no, no, guys, you got this all wrong. It's just a

toy. Really. I entered the Whizzer Toy Contest and I'm taking my kite to New York," Vincent said.

"What kind of kite has all those wires?" the guard asked.

"A windless kite," Vincent said proudly.

"A windless kite?"

"Yeah, a windless kite. As in, it doesn't need any wind," Vincent said, confident that the guard would understand.

"Yeah, right," the guard said.

"No, really. I'll show you," Vincent said as he started to stand up, only to be shoved back in his chair by two burly guards.

"Frank, why don't you check it out," the guard said to the man standing closest to the bag. Everyone stepped away from Frank.

Frank carefully unzipped the bag.

"Yeah, it kind of looks like a kite," Frank said.

"All right, kid," the guard said, "let's see this windless kite."

Vincent cautiously stood up. He walked to his bag and took out the kite and the spool of speaker wire.

"You may want to stand back a little," Vincent warned Frank.

Vincent laid the kite on the floor and walked backward, letting out about ten feet of speaker wire. He looked up and noticed that a large crowd of people had gathered around him. There were now over a hundred people waiting to see his windless kite. Most of them looked worried. So did Vincent.

"Here it goes." The crowd winced as Vincent pushed the green button. Vincent winced, too.

The kite started hissing. Then a few sparks jumped from the guitar string to the shiny kite, and it soared high up into the air as if it had caught a strong breeze.

The crowd gasped. So did Vincent. The kite was glowing blue along the edges. Vincent let out more wire and the kite soared high in the airport terminal. The crowd was getting larger. One little boy turned to his dad and asked if Vincent was magic.

Suddenly the kite darted to the left. Then to the right. The kite became a silvery blue blur as it darted here and there. The crowd started clapping. People were taking pictures. They thought Vincent was putting on a fantastic aerial show. But Vincent knew something had gone wrong. Something had gone horribly wrong.

The kite was now diving toward the crowd, and the applause turned to screams as people dove out of the way. Vincent pulled hard on the speaker wire and the kite soared back toward the ceiling. Lightning shot from the tail of the kite to the airport lights high above the people. The lights burst. Vincent quickly gave the kite slack and it reversed course, darting back toward the fleeing crowd. Vincent pulled hard on the speaker wire once again, and the kite flew just above the crowd, zapping the heads of several tall bald men. Vincent reached down and pushed the off button. The kite instantly fell to the floor.

"Sorry. It's a prototype," Vincent said with a smile.

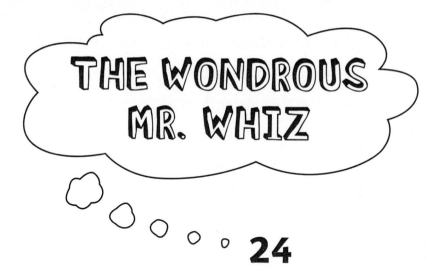

THE WONDROUS MR. WHIZ

24

Howard G. Whiz was thirty-seven years old when his father died. Even though they hadn't spoken in years, the news of his father's death devastated him.

Howard's father had left no will. So, as an only child, Howard inherited his father's massive fortune, a fortune built on young Howard's inventions. Howard also inherited the Carlisle, a six-story gothic mansion located in the heart of New York City, across the street from the Metropolitan Museum of Art.

Shortly after the funeral, Howard closed the Whizzer Toy factory and moved into his father's house. For the next three years he lived alone on the top floor of the Carlisle. Then, the morning of his fortieth birthday he called four former Whizzer Toy employees: a computer programmer, an artist, a brilliant physicist named Fayman, and a poet named Earl. He invited this select group of former employees to a dinner where he unveiled his plans to launch a new and improved Whizzer Toys. Howard G. Whiz, with the help of his longtime assistant Calli and the four talented employees, launched one of the most spectacularly successful toy companies in history.

The new Whizzer Toy Company operated for the next forty-three years out of the first five floors of the Carlisle. In his desire to cut out greedy middlemen,

Howard decided to sell his inventions directly to his customers through a catalog called the Wondrous Whizzer Wishbook. Howard insisted that only "the most amazing magical toys" be included in the Wishbook. He put out twenty editions over the years, but it had been a long time since the last Wishbook was published, and because of Howard's age, many people feared it would be the last.

Aunt Bonnie collected salt and pepper

shakers. She had thousands of them on display in her

apartment.

"And I got this one from your Uncle Ernie. Oh boy,

did he love to fish. See, the salt and pepper comes out

of the top of the bobbers." Aunt Bonnie laughed as she

held two oversized ceramic salt and pepper shakers

shaped like fishing bobbers. "And these were my first

rooster shakers. Of course now I have hundreds of roosters, chickens, turkeys—you name a bird and I've got a salt and pepper shaker of it."

"It's an amazing collection," Stella said.

"Thanks, hon. Now, do you have enough blankets, dear? Are you going to be warm enough? It is so much fun to have people staying with me. I want to make sure you're warm enough. No one has used those back bedrooms in, well . . . in a long time."

Vincent looked out the window as their taxi pulled up. "We have to go to dinner, Aunt Bonnie. Our cab is here."

"Okay. Now here is the key. I can't stay up late like you young kids. Just come in and make yourself at home. My home is your home. You know that, Vincent. You know that."

"I know. Thank you," Vincent said.

Vincent and Stella walked toward the door.

"I will be gone by the time you kids get up in the morning. I like to be at the museum by five thirty. I make the coffee. But I will meet you at the show by eight. I'm so excited, Vincent. I wouldn't miss it. I know you are going to do great. Just great, hon." She kissed Vincent on the cheek.

Vincent and Stella got out of the taxicab at the corner of Fifth Avenue and 78th Street. Vincent looked up at the ornate building and asked the cab driver if he was sure this was the right place.

"This is it," the cabbie said. "This is the Carlisle, home to world-famous toymaker Howard G. Whiz."

"I can't believe it," Vincent said. "I've walked past this building nearly every day of my life. I had no idea Mr. Whiz lived here."

"It's as big as a hotel," Stella said.

They walked up to the front door and rang the bell.

"Hello, you must be Vincent," Calli said, greeting them.

"Yes, and this is my sister Stella. We're here for the toy contest dinner," Vincent said.

"We've been expecting you. Come on in. My name is Calli Callosum and I will be your host this evening. Welcome to Whizzer Toys," Calli said as she stuck name tags on both of them.

"Let me introduce you to the other contestants." Calli led them up a large staircase to a ballroom that overlooked Central Park. A dozen people, children and their parents, sat around a table in the middle of the room.

"Everyone, please allow me to introduce Vincent Shadow and his sister Stella. Vincent has invented a windless kite that, by the way, Vincent, we are all very eager to see," Calli said.

Vincent smiled nervously and Calli continued the introductions. "The twins here are Seamus and Liam O'Toole. They invented hockey skates that allow you to skate on air. Very cool," Calli said. "And this is Gabriella Guzzi. Gabby has invented a sprinkler toy she calls Elli-Squirt. It's a very cute elephant that, well, let's just say it's full of surprises." Gabby smiled and nodded in agreement.

"Next to Gabby is Isabel. Isabel has invented a musical pacifier that plays music when it is in the baby's mouth. Very clever. Alli here has invented a remote-controlled Slinky that doesn't need stairs to walk. And last, but not least, this is George Spinowski, Junior. George's invention is the Story Time Toilet Seat, and I don't need to tell you what that does," Calli said as she let out a giggle.

"Hello," Vincent said.

"Well, you two have a seat and dinner will be served shortly," Calli said.

"Excuse me, ma'am," George Jr.'s dad, George Spinowski Sr., said. "When will Mr. Whiz be joining us?"

"Oh no. Oh no, I will be your host this evening," Calli said.

"Well," George Sr. continued, "isn't that a little rude? We came a long way to be here, and little George Jr. would like to meet the great Mr. Howard G. Whiz."

"I am so sorry, Mr. Spinowski, but Mr. Whiz was otherwise occupied this evening. But rest assured, little George Jr. will get a chance to meet Mr. Whiz at the Toy Fair competition tomorrow," Calli said as she walked away.

"So, Vincent. A windless kite, eh?" George Sr. said. "What does it do?"

"It flies, you know, without wind," Vincent said.

"What, do you have a fan attached to the kite or something?" George Jr. asked.

"No. No fan. Actually, it has no moving parts," Vincent said.

"Yeah, no moving parts," the two Georges said in unison, and laughed until they realized Vincent wasn't kidding.

"How did you do that?" George Sr. asked, now sounding a little nervous.

"You'll have to wait and find out tomorrow," Stella said.

Waiters started to bring out the food. And they kept bringing it. Course after course. Vincent was completely stuffed by the end of the eighth course and decided to pass on dessert.

"Okay, if everyone will follow me, we would like to get a few pictures of all the young inventors with their spectacular inventions," Calli said as she led them into an adjacent room where the inventions had been carefully placed on a table.

"Wow, that looks so cool," Liam said as he ran over to Vincent's kite.

Seamus tried to pick up Alli's remote-controlled Slinky, but got a shock.

"Please, boys, please put the inventions down," Calli said. "We don't want anyone's invention to break before tomorrow's competition."

"So this is the kite?" George Sr. asked.

"Yup."

"I see you have wire instead of string. What, this big box zaps the kite somehow?" George Sr. asked.

"Yeah, something like that," Vincent said as he grabbed the high voltage spool out of Mr. Spinowski's hands.

"Be careful, Vincent," Stella whispered in his ear. "I don't trust those Spinowskis."

"Okay, you with the kite, could you kneel in front of the larger boy in the red shirt?" the photographer said.

"Great. And you two"—the photographer pointed to Liam and Seamus—"could you kneel down in front, too? Great. Now move closer. A little closer everyone, come on, no one here bites. Good," the photographer said as he started snapping pictures.

"Great. Now let's get a picture of each of you alone with your invention. You," the photographer pointed to Alli. "Come on over here. Great. Perfect." He snapped a few shots of Alli and the remote-controlled Slinky in front of the window.

"All right, let's get the kite boy next. Please come on over here," the photographer said.

Vincent stood up and carefully held his kite out in front of him. The kite's tail trailed behind as he walked toward the photographer. George Jr. looked over to his father. His father motioned with his foot. George Jr. shrugged his shoulders. He had no idea what his father was trying to tell him. His father pointed down. George Jr. looked down and saw the tail of the kite trailing behind Vincent. George Jr. stepped on it, and the kite came to an instant stop. Unfortunately, Vincent did not. The kite ripped in half. Vincent spun around to see what was wrong, got tangled in the kite tail, and began to fall. He landed on the kite, breaking it into pieces.

Stella ran to his side. Vincent didn't say a word. He just lay there. The kite was a tangled mess.

"Oh no!" people yelled. The Spinowskis were smiling. With Vincent out of the contest, George Sr. thought his son was sure to win. A summer internship at Whizzer Toys would provide George Jr. with plenty of opportunities to steal inventions from the great Howard G. Whiz.

"Oh boy, oh boy," Calli said kneeling down next to Vincent. "This has never happened before. Maybe you can glue it back together."

"I'm sure we can fix it," Stella said.

Vincent said nothing.

"Are you okay?" Stella asked.

Vincent said nothing. He stood up. He bunched the tangled mess into a ball, walked over to the trash can, and threw the kite away.

"Are you okay, Vincent?" Stella asked again.

Vincent nodded yes and then asked Calli, "Which way to the bathroom?"

"Down the hall," she said. "Take the first left and then a quick right."

Vincent couldn't believe his bad luck. It had taken almost every minute of every day for the last two weeks to build his kite. There was no way he could build another one by the next morning. Devastated, he slowly wandered down the hallway.

Maybe it just wasn't meant to be, he thought. *Maybe I am not meant to be an inventor.*

Vincent was dazed. He thought he had taken a left, but maybe it was a right. Or a left and then a right. The hallway seemed to go on forever. He couldn't remember what Calli had said, and he wasn't quite sure where he was now.

THE ROOM OF FIRSTS

26

People collect all kinds of things: stamps, baseball cards, spoons, and even salt and pepper shakers. Howard Whiz collected inventions. He had one of the first pedal bicycles, invented in 1818. He had one of Edison's first lightbulbs from 1879. He had the first drinking straw (1888), movie camera (1891), paper clip (1899), box of crayons (1903), and hair dryer

(1920). He even had one of Les Paul's electric guitars, which he first built in 1941.

Vincent couldn't believe his eyes. He had accidentally stumbled into Howard G. Whiz's private museum. It was a large room with shelves on all four walls. The shelves held some of the greatest inventions of the twentieth century. Hundreds of them, each with a brass plate inscribed with the invention, the inventor, and the date of the invention. The Monopoly game, patented by Charles B. Darrow in 1935. The skateboard, built by Bill and Mark Richards in 1958. The teddy bear, invented by Morris Michtom in 1902, Itch Toilet Paper, invented by Mike Spinowski, George Jr.'s grandfather, in 1935, and the Slinky, invented by Richard James in 1943.

Four large, red curtains were hung in the middle of the room, concealing what Vincent imagined to be the most magnificent invention of all. The curtains were surrounded by the other inventions that were too large to fit on the shelves. There was a 1938 Triumph Speed Twin motorcycle, invented by Edward Turner. Even a diving suit invented in 1921 by the magician Harry Houdini.

Vincent walked slowly from invention to invention, reading every name and date. Then he saw it. The invention he had seen in the basement of the Met. The one Stella had cranked up. It had been cleaned up and several new pieces had been added to the device, but Vincent knew it was—

"One of Tesla's greatest inventions," a voice said behind him.

Vincent turned around to see a frail-looking old man dressed all in white.

"Mr. Whiz? Sir?" Vincent said, startled. "I'm sorry, sir. I was, I was just looking for the bathroom."

Vincent noticed the kite on Mr. Whiz's tie.

"It's an honor to meet you, sir."

"No, Vincent. The honor is all mine."

Vincent couldn't believe the great Howard G. Whiz knew his name.

"I see you are admiring one of the latest additions to my collection," Howard said, leaning on his cane.

"Yes, it's beautiful."

"You know, I met him once when I was a little boy," Howard said, motioning to a photo of Tesla on the wall. "Yes, he had striking eyes. They were a brilliant blue. Most unusual," Howard said.

"Wow. What was he like?" Vincent asked.

"Charming. Brilliant. Too brilliant for me to actually understand." Howard chuckled. "I didn't understand most of what Tesla said, but I think you would have, Vincent. I just saw your kite on TV. It's brilliant, Vincent. Just brilliant."

Vincent didn't know what Mr. Whiz was talking about. His kite hadn't been on TV.

"And my cousin Dennis has great things to say about you," Howard added.

"Do you mind if I ask you what's behind the curtain over there?" Vincent said.

"Ah, that, my boy, is one of Tesla's most ambitious

and misunderstood inventions," Howard said. "It isn't done yet, but maybe you will be around this summer to help me finish it."

"I saw this invention at the Met, but it didn't have all of these pieces."

"Yes, it's taken me quite some time to piece it all together."

"What is it, Mr. Whiz?"

"You are looking at one of the first vacuum tube Tesla coils," Howard answered.

"Does it work?"

"It sure does," Howard replied. "Most everything Tesla built, worked. It's criminal, what they did to him. Just criminal. He's given us all so much, and we let him die penniless and hungry. They called him crazy at the end of his life. Crazy because he had the courage to create. People are too quick to dismiss what they don't understand."

"How did you find all the pieces?"

"It wasn't easy, Vincent. Tesla lived in several different hotels. Often he would move, leaving notebooks and prototypes behind. I've spent the last twelve years scouring New York and looking for Tesla prototypes, trying to put his collection back together," Howard said.

"Is this a—" Hundreds of glowing bubbles filled the room as Vincent touched the glass tube attached to the Tesla coil. Vincent could hear the blood rushing to his head. The room began to spin. *Not now*, he thought. The bubbles glowed brightly against the now completely black room. Vincent waved his hand in the air in an effort to pop dozens of bubbles that seemed to be floating around him. A strange device came into focus. It looked like his Pop Tunz bubble blowers attached to the vacuum tube Tesla coil.

"That's it!" he muttered. The solution to Pop Tunz

had been right in front of him. "The vacuum tube keeps the high voltage from getting out of control."

"Right! Absolutely right! See, I knew you would understand Tesla's work. I knew it!" Howard said.

Vincent could see the solution clearly. But the solution and the bubbles were the only things he could see. The rest of the world was dark.

"Are you okay, Vincent?" Howard asked.

"Yes sir, I . . . I just got something in my eyes. Would you mind showing me how to get back to the group, sir? I have a lot of work to do before tomorrow."

FAME

27

Erik Norsted e-mailed the pictures of "this amazing kid and his windless kite" to his wife. Charlie and Maria Girsch had also taken pictures of "some kid flying a kite inside the airport!" Rollie Black shot a video of Vincent and posted it online. Someone recognized him in the video and by 6:00 PM Vincent was famous.

By 8:00 PM more than twenty-five million people had seen the photos and watched the video of Vincent and

his kite. Reporters were camped out in the Shadows' front yard, wanting to know more about the amazing young inventor already being hailed as the next Thomas Edison. It seemed like everyone had seen the video. Everyone but Vincent. As Vincent blindly felt his way down the hall, trying to get back to Stella, he had no knowledge of his newfound fame.

"Vincent, are you all right? I was getting worried about you," Stella said.

"I'm great. I met Mr. Whiz!" Vincent said.

Stella looked down the hallway.

"What was he like? Was he nice?"

"He was charming. But I had an idea and, well . . . well, I need your help getting out of here. We have a lot to do."

"No problem. Here, I grabbed your kite out of the garbage. You know, I get the feeling the Spinowskis tripped you on purpose." Stella looked over to the table and both generations of Spinowskis were wearing stupid grins.

"Oh, there you are, Mr. Shadow," Calli said. "I reread the rules and unfortunately we are unable to grant you an extension. You need to fix your invention by the time the contest starts at 8:00 AM tomorrow morning or I'm afraid you will be disqualified."

"Isn't there anything you can—" Stella started to ask, but Vincent cut her off.

"No," Vincent said as he held the tangled mess that

used to be idea No. 50. "Don't worry about it. We'll be there tomorrow morning at 8:00 AM. Do you have a bag I can put this in?"

Stella looked at the food-soaked, tangled mess in Vincent's hand and said, "How are you going to fix it in time, Vincent?"

"Come on. We have to go shopping before we go to the lab," Vincent said.

"Lab? What lab?"

DANGER BOY

28

"Hey, Vincent! Long time no see," the clerk said from behind the counter.

"Hey, Googie. How's it going?" Vincent asked.

"Good, man, good. Dude, I haven't seen your dad in here for months. He hasn't stopped playing his guitar, has he?"

"No. He's just been real busy with work." Vincent didn't want to explain that his dad had met a woman online and destroyed his life by moving them to Minnesota.

"What can I do you for?"

"I need—I mean, my dad needs some new vacuum tubes for his guitar amp."

"Cool, cool. So he's still playing." Googie walked out from behind the counter. "Here, he likes the Groove Tubes the best."

"Great," Vincent said. "Give me three Groove Tubes."

With his new Groove Tubes in hand, Vincent led the way.

"What are we doing here?" Stella asked as they stood across the street from their old house.

"We need to get in to my old room."

"Your old room? Why?"

"I have some things hidden there," Vincent said. "Things that might help us win the contest."

"Hidden things? What kind of hidden things?" Stella asked.

"You know, invention things."

"Invention things?"

"Yeah, like hidden-invention-lab kinds of things," Vincent said.

"What? Like you have the Batcave hidden in your old room?"

"Something like that."

"Well then, maybe we should shoot our rappelling ropes around the chimney and swing through your bedroom window."

"Come on, Stella. I'm serious."

"I have an idea," Stella said. "Why don't we just knock on the door?"

"Yeah, then what?"

"I don't know." Stella started walking across the street. "I'm sure you'll think of something—inventor boy." Stella rang the doorbell.

Mrs. Zimmerman opened the door. "Hello. Can I help you?"

"Hi. I know this is going to sound a little strange, but my sister and I use to live here and we were—"

"Oh my, you're him, aren't you? You're the kid on TV with the kite. We saw you flying your kite in that airport. Amazing," Mrs. Zimmerman said. "Oh, my son Timmy has some friends over for his birthday. I know they would love to meet you. Do you have time to come in?"

Vincent looked at Stella. "Sure," they said together.

"You can set your bag down here. Timmy and the rest of the kids are in the kitchen."

A dozen children were huddled around a cake that read "HAPPY 7TH BIRTHDAY DANGER BOY."

Danger Boy, known to some

as Timmy Zimmerman, had always wanted to be a stuntman. And that had always terrified his mother. At the tender age of two, little Timmy slid down an entire flight of stairs headfirst on his pillowcase. At the age of three, Timmy had jumped off the top bunk of his bed and landed—headfirst—in a pile of clothes. His mom bought him a helmet for his fourth birthday.

By the time he turned five, Timmy was building makeshift ramps and performing death-defying stunts with his bike. The summer of his sixth birthday, he jumped his bike over Katelyn Meyers, Katelyn's brother Nick, and their dog Buddy. He earned the nickname "Danger Boy" that summer.

"Timmy, this is—oh, I didn't get your name," Mrs. Zimmerman said.

"Vincent Shadow."

"This is Vincent. He's that boy who invented that windless kite."

"Happy Birthday, Timmy—or should I say—Danger Boy."

"What are you doing at my birthday party?"

"Well, I actually used to live here and—"

"And we thought it would be fun to see who lives here now," Stella interjected.

"Did you bring the kite?" Danger Boy asked.

"No. No kite. But," Vincent was desperately trying to think of a way to get upstairs, "I bet we could invent something together."

"Oh, yeah? Like what?" Danger Boy challenged.

"Well, I could show you how to build a crossbow out of an old shoe, clothes hangers, and a couple of pencils. I bet we could find that stuff up in your room," Vincent said.

"Sounds lame," Danger Boy said.

"Yeah. Lame, dude," the other kids chimed in.

"Aahhhh, okay." Vincent looked around the kitchen.

"What if I make fireballs shoot from your birthday cake?"

The boy sitting next to Timmy started to say, "You can't do—" but Timmy pushed his hand up against his friend's chest to silence him.

"Show me," Danger Boy said.

"Okay. I'm gonna need to cut a piece of your cake here." Vincent cut a piece of birthday cake and put it on a paper plate. He stuck a birthday candle in the middle of the cake.

"I need matches and a large glass bowl."

"Oh, are you sure this is safe?" Mrs. Zimmerman asked as she handed Vincent matches and a large bowl.

"Good point. Remember, guys, not to try this at home without your—"

"Get on with it," Danger Boy demanded.

Vincent set the timer for forty-five seconds, lit the candle, and placed the glass bowl over the cake with the lit candle. He closed the microwave door and pushed START.

Danger Boy held his breath as he watched the cake spin around inside the microwave. Soon the candle flame flickered and then a fireball shot from the candle and seemed to stick to the top of the bowl . . . still glowing. Then another fireball, followed by another, and yet another. Soon there was a massive fireball trapped inside the glass bowl.

"Awesome," Danger Boy said as the microwave beeped and went black. "Do it again!"

"Did you like that?" Vincent asked.

"Yeah!" the kids yelled.

Even Stella was amazed. "How did you do that?"

"That's nothing," Vincent said. He pointed to Danger Boy's Harley-Davidson T-shirt. "I see you like motorcycles."

"Yeah," Danger Boy answered.

"You should see his room. It's covered with motorcycle posters," the boy sitting next to Danger Boy said.

"I'd love to see the posters in your room. Can you show me?" Vincent asked.

"Yeah, that would be cool," Stella quickly added.

"Later. Come on. More fireworks," Danger Boy said.

"I bet you have more cool motorcycle T-shirts in your closet. I would love to see them." Vincent was desperate to get upstairs. Time was running out.

"Shadow, on with the show," Danger Boy insisted.

"Right. Right. Ah, who wants to see a—a hydrogen-powered rocket? I mean, who wants to see a crazy, high-powered, dangerously fast rocket?"

"We do! We do!" Danger Boy and his friends were now surrounding Vincent.

"Do you have any hydrogen peroxide in the house, Mrs. Zimmerman?" Vincent asked.

"I don't know. There might be some up in the closet."

"Great." Vincent let out a sigh of relief. "Danger Boy, you take us upstairs and we'll build you the most powerful, most dangerous birthday rocket you've ever seen."

Danger Boy was halfway up the stairs before Vincent could finish his sentence. Vincent grabbed the bag with the kite remains and Groove Tubes, and he and Stella followed Danger Boy up the stairs.

"Okay, here's the closet. Now what?"

"You go downstairs and we'll be down in ten minutes with the craziest, fastest rocket you've ever—" Vincent hadn't even finished his sentence and Danger Boy was gone.

"What are you going to do with the hydrogen peroxide?" Stella asked.

"Nothing," Vincent said as he put it back in the closet. "But we're upstairs. . . ."

LAB PARTNERS

29

Vincent reached into the dark and pulled
on the rope.

"Welcome to my lab."

"Oh my gosh, Vincent." Stella looked around the room at all the equipment and prototypes. "This is incredible!"

She touched a sketch. "What is all this?"

"This is the Batcave. I'll have to give you the details

some other time, but you know those headaches I get?"

Stella nodded as she read the labels on various jars of experiments.

"Well, they aren't really headaches. They're more like inspiration. Intense ideas." Vincent realized he hadn't talked about this with anyone but his mother.

"Intense ideas?" Stella asked.

"Yeah. I see toys. Toys that don't exist. My mom and I built this lab so I could try and build them. But no one can know about this, Stella."

"Come on, Batman. You know your secret is safe with me. But what if Danger Boy and his mom come looking for us?" Stella asked.

"As long as we're quiet, they'll never find us in here. They'll probably assume we couldn't build the rocket and left."

"Yeah, well, we may have an easier time building the

rocket than fixing this kite." Stella pulled the broken, balled-up mess from the bag.

"We're not going to fix it," Vincent said. "We're going to build something even better. My mom and I spent years working on bubbles that release sound when they pop. But I've never been able to get them to work. They need high voltage. But the high voltage makes the bubble solution uncontrollable." Vincent pointed to the scorched remains from his last night in the lab.

"So, maybe we'd be better off getting one of these to work," Stella said as she picked up a basketball with a built-in targeting system. "This is cool," she said as she aimed the ball.

"Thanks. That's the Bullz-I Basketball. Look—" Vincent pointed to a sketch in his notebook. "All this time the answer was right in front of me. Tonight, Mr. Whiz showed me a Tesla invention that looked just like this."

"Hey, that looks like the thing we saw at the Met."

"It *is* the thing we saw at the Met. That thing is actually a high-powered Tesla coil with a vacuum tube." Vincent flipped to the sketch of his Pop Tunz device. "If I connect the Tesla coil from my kite to my Pop Tunz device . . ." Vincent drew a Tesla coil on the tail end of the sketch of his bubble blower and then reached into the bag from the music store and pulled out the vacuum tubes. "And I attach the Groove Tubes to the front nozzle, maybe, just maybe, the bubbles will work."

"And then the bubbles will play a sound?"

"I hope so," Vincent said.

"Hey!" Stella pointed to Snonkey the Great across the room. "You did take Anna's animals!"

"All in the name of science." Vincent smiled.

"What do these do?" Stella pointed to prototypes for Art 3-D, Sonic Snorkelz, Sno-zuka, Sketch 'n' Sculpt, and Alarminalz.

"That one lets you draw in 3D. That one lets you talk underwater. That shoots snowballs. That lets you draw with growing ink, and that's an alarm clock," Vincent said. "Actually, grab that Alarminalz." He pointed to the stuffed lion.

"This?" Stella held it up.

"Yeah. It has an alarm clock built into it. We can use that to wake us up early. We're gonna have to sneak out of here before Danger Boy and his friends wake up."

Vincent unwrapped the three glass Groove Tubes and the Tesla coil from the windless kite and set them on the table in the middle of the room.

"These inventions are great, Vincent," Stella said as she continued to look at all the drawings of inventions taped to the walls.

"Thanks. Can you grab one of those gun-looking things from the top shelf?"

"I was always better at writing than drawing. Is this the thing you want?" Stella pointed to a Pop Tunz bubble-blowing prototype.

"Yeah, that one will work."

Vincent slid a large box out from under the table and pulled out his catcher's mask and pads. "What's that stuff for?" Stella asked.

"It's going to be a long night, Sis," Vincent replied.

Stella smiled. That was the second time today Vincent had called her Sis.

TOY FAIR

30

BEEP BEEP

BEEP BEEP

BEEP BEEP

Howard sat up in his chair and rubbed his eyes. He looked across the room at the alarm clock. 5:30 AM. He must have fallen asleep at his drawing table. Again.

BEEP BEEP

BEEP BEEP

BEEP BEEP

Howard G. Whiz walked across the room and pushed the off button on the alarm clock.

Toy Fair was the one time a year that toy companies, from all over the world, gathered in New York to unveil their latest creations. And, most importantly, Toy Fair was the time a year that Howard selected the winner of the annual Whizzer Toys invention contest.

Howard took a new white tie from his closet and sat back down at his drawing table. He stared out the window and thought about the Toy Fair. Then he thought about the contest, the kids, and their wonderful inventions. He grabbed a paintbrush, opened three jars of paint, and prepared to create that day's tie.

This was Howard's routine every morning for the

last 22,438 mornings. But this morning Howard did something he had never done. He smiled, screwed the lids back on the jars of paint, and decided to wear a completely white tie.

"Perfect," he said.

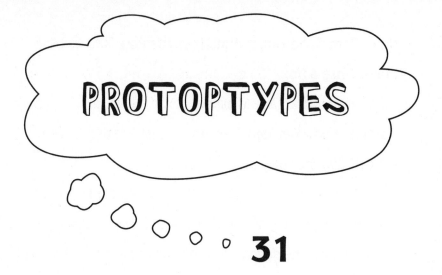

PROTOPTYPES

31

The Alarminalz's roar woke Stella. She opened her eyes and looked up at Vincent, still hard at work.

"What time is it?" she asked.

Vincent looked at his watch. "It's eight thirty."

Stella jumped up. "We're late! You'll be disqualified!"

"I'm almost ready. I had a ton of ideas hit me last night. Talk about bad timing. It was hard to get this thing done." Vincent carefully set the Pop Tunz bubble blower into a box.

"Does it work?" Stella asked.

"I hope so. I decided I better not test it. I didn't want to wake Danger Boy and company."

Vincent placed three glass jars of black liquid into the box. Stella carefully opened the lab door and peered out of the closet. The seven-year-olds were all still asleep.

After Vincent and Stella had disappeared, the boys had looked for them for about two minutes before losing interest. Then, they had stayed up late eating pizza and bragging about the stunts they would perform when they were older.

Making as little noise as was humanly possible, they stepped over the boys in sleeping bags and avoided getting too close to Danger Boy, who slept hugging a brand new cherry-red Whizzer Board 4000 with the bow still on it.

THE SHOW MUST GO ON

32

Seamus and Liam skated off the stage
and the crowd erupted in applause. They loved Seamus
and Liam and they loved their Airblades invention.

"Has Vincent arrived yet?" Howard Whiz asked Calli.

There were three thousand people in the audience.
And they were all there to see Vincent Shadow and his
amazing windless kite.

"No. I'm sorry, sir, but no one has heard from him. It

looks like Vincent is going to miss the contest. We only have two contestants left."

George Spinowski Jr. felt sick as he looked out at the sea of people. He didn't like crowds.

"Okay, George, you're up," Calli said.

His stomach hurt. He was sure he was going to be sick.

"Can I go last, Ms. Callosum?" George asked.

"Sure, George," Calli said. "That means you're up next, Gabby."

Gabby connected the Elli-Squirt sprinkler toy to a garden hose and walked onto the stage.

Norton, Vibs, and the girls had taken a late flight to New York the previous night, hoping to surprise Vincent. But Vibs was currently focused on the surprise Gabby had in store for the audience.

"Is that a garden hose?" Vibs asked.

"Yeah, I think it is," Norton said.

"Well, they aren't going to let her use that in here . . . are they?"

Gabby started to introduce her product. "This is my invention. It's a sprinkler toy, but not like any sprinkler toy you have ever . . ."

"Yeah, I think they're going to let her use it," Norton said.

"Norton, this is silk." Vibs touched her blouse. "This cannot get wet. We're moving!" Vibs stood up and marched toward the back.

"Come on, girls," Norton said to Gwen and Anna. "Your mom doesn't want to get wet." Norton stood up and followed Vibs to the back of the hall.

"Norton! Norton!"

Norton looked around. He heard someone calling his name but couldn't tell where it was coming from.

"Norton, honey! Over here!" He looked to his left and saw Aunt Bonnie sitting with a group of schoolkids.

"It was the only seat left." She shrugged. "I'm so glad you made it. Vincent is going to be *thrilled* to see you."

"Have you seen Vincent yet?" Norton asked.

"No. Not yet. Maybe he's next. You better get to your seat."

Norton nodded in agreement and rushed after Vibs and the girls just as the crowd stood up and began clapping.

Gabby picked up her sprinkler toy and walked off the stage.

"Amazing, Gabby. Just amazing. The ending gets me every time," Calli said.

"Okay, George, your turn. Knock 'em dead."

George Jr. took a few steps onto the stage and then quickly turned around and began to walk off when his father grabbed him by the arm.

"I need you to win this contest. Now suck it up. Get out there and win this thing," George Sr. said.

"But Dad, my stomach—"

His dad shot him a look that he knew all too well. George Jr. turned around and walked to the middle of the stage as his stomach gurgled. He pulled a sheet off a shiny white toilet.

"He invented a toilet," someone shouted from the crowd.

"Maybe it's a remote-controlled toilet!" another yelled.

The crowd laughed.

"This is my invention," George Jr. said as he pointed to the toilet seat with one hand while holding his stomach with the other. "I call it the

Story Time Toilet Seat. When the, ah, the user sits down on the toilet, the seat will tell a story."

George was extremely nervous. Everyone in the first row could hear George's stomach.

George Jr. continued, "My toilet seat is completely wireless. The ah, ah, the user can download their favorite story and listen to it while they do their business."

George Jr. had sweat running down his face. He started to shake. He wasn't sure he could continue.

BLOUP BLOUP BLOUP. His stomach bubbled.

George looked over to his dad for help, but his dad was still wearing "the look."

"Now I will demonstrate how it works." George carefully lifted the toilet seat and sat down.

The toilet seat began telling one of George's favorite stories: "Now I don't want to put all the blame on my parents, but if you grew up with a name like Furious Jones, you too would have—"

"I can't hear it," one man yelled.

"Turn it up," another yelled.

Calli walked out onstage and handed George Jr. a microphone. George held the microphone next to the toilet seat. The story bellowed out over the auditorium loudspeaker and the crowd clapped. Soon they rose to their feet and the applause strengthened. George Jr. smiled. They loved it. He wished his grandfather could see it. George Jr. was so excited as he walked off the stage that he forgot all about his nerves.

BUBBLE BOY

33

Howard Whiz walked onto the stage and the crowd rose to their feet. They clapped, hooted, and hollered as Howard slowly made his way to the microphone.

"Thank you, thank you," he said to the crowd. They clapped louder.

"Thank you all for coming. This contest, and being

here with these young inventors and all of you, well, it's the best. Just the best."

They clapped even louder.

"Thank you," Howard said. "Through hard work and courage, I have been fortunate to spend every day of my life doing what I love most: inventing toys. And today, you had the chance to meet some very special kids who had the courage to follow their dreams. And their dreams led them here today." The crowd was still on its feet. "One of those talented kids will have the opportunity to spend the summer with me, and together we will work hard to bring you the toys of tomorrow."

"Where's Vincent?" someone yelled.

"Let's see the kite," another yelled.

The crowd became restless.

"I'm sorry, folks. I know many of you came here today expecting to see Mr. Shadow's kite. Well," Howard paused. "Well, there has been a change in plans, and unfortunately Mr. Shadow and his kite will not be part of the contest today. So, without further ado, this year's Whizzer Toys invention contest winner is—" Howard was suddenly distracted by a black bubble that was floating inches from his face. He reached out and popped it with his finger.

FOO.

Another bubble floated down toward the stage. Howard poked it.

BEE.

"Did you hear that?" Howard asked.

A murmur swept through the crowd. They didn't know what was going on.

"What is Howard pointing at?" Vibs asked Norton.

"I'm not sure," Norton said. And Norton didn't care. He was worried about Vincent. Now dozens of black bubbles were falling toward the stage. Howard was popping them.

BEE.

ZOO.

BEE.

FOO.

A single giant bubble now floated down toward Howard. He popped it with the microphone, and the word *FOOBEEZOOBEE* echoed through the auditorium.

"It's Vincent Shadow!" a man yelled, pointing to the catwalk high above the stage.

The spectators rose to their feet as Vincent grabbed a rope and slid down onto the stage.

Vincent's class from Central Middle School in New York had seen Vincent on the news and had come to support him. And now they were all on their feet chanting, "VIN-CENT VIN-CENT VIN-CENT."

Vincent held the Pop Tunz bubble blower high in the air and unleashed dozens of bubbles from the jar marked "electric guitar." The bubbles floated out over the crowd and burst into a full-throttle, funk-punk guitar solo. The crowd went wild. Vincent had done it. After years of trying, his bubbles were real—and people loved them.

Vincent switched jars and blew dozens of black bubbles onstage. Howard Whiz, with his white suit, white hair, white cane, and all-white tie, was now running around the stage popping bubbles like a little boy.

FOO.

BEE.

ZOO.

BEE.

FOO.

BEE.

ZOO.

BEE.

The crowd began chanting, "FOO-BEE-ZOO-BEE, FOO-BEE-ZOO-BEE," as Howard chased the bubbles.

Howard took Vincent by the hand and said, "I give you the Whizzer Toy contest winner: Vincent Shadow!"

The crowd began rushing the stage. Everyone was pushing and pulling, trying to get close to Vincent and trying to pop the bubbles.

Norton, Vibs, Gwen, and Anna made their way through the crowd.

"Dad, you're here!"

"That was amazing, Vincent. How did you do that?"

"Long story, Dad."

"Not bad, Vincent," Gwen said.

"What? What was that?"

Gwen smiled. "I said not bad—Vincent."

Someone tapped Vincent on his shoulder. He turned around to find Jeff Benz and several of his former Central Middle School classmates.

"Way to go, Bubble Boy," Jeff said.

Bubble Boy? Vincent thought. *Well, it beats Wigboy.*

Howard G. Whiz walked up and shook hands with Norton and Vibs.

"You must be Vincent's parents."

"We are," Vibs quickly answered.

"Well, I don't have to tell you how special he is. Vincent, I would like to invite you to work with me this summer at Whizzer Toys, if it's okay with your parents, of course," Howard said.

Vincent looked at his father. "Of course it's okay," Norton said.

"We've always been so proud of Vincent," Vibs added.

"Well, then, Mr. Shadow, I will see you in a few weeks." Vincent nodded and looked at Stella.

"We did it!"

More toys.

More pressure.

More surprises and
crazy inventions!

Turn the page for a sneak peek
at the fun and toy-filled sequel to

Vincent Shadow:
Toy Inventor

Coming Fall 2011.

BUNK BEDS

1

New York, New York

All parents keep a secret list of mistakes

—a top-secret list of regrets that they share only with other parents. And while some of those lists may include the purchase of bunk beds, Nancy Zimmerman is, perhaps, the only parent to put the purchase of her son's bunk bed at the very top of the list.

Timmy Zimmerman, better known as Danger Boy

to his friends and family, discovered his love of stunts shortly after his mother purchased his bunk bed. The bed had played a major role in many of his death-defying stunts over the years. But today Timmy was preparing to take danger to a new level.

Timmy carefully removed the plastic motorcycle models from his bookcase and leaned the empty bookcase against his bunk bed. Then he positioned his bike jump at the base of the bookcase. Now the back of the bookcase formed a solid ramp to the bike jump.

Timmy duct-taped a pillow to his old skateboard and climbed to the top bunk. He looked down the ramp and figured he would be traveling thirty or fifty miles per hour by the time he reached the jump. Professional stuntmen always take safety precautions and Timmy believed he was nothing if not professional. So he strapped on his foam bike helmet and mounted the skateboard.

Timmy was lying headfirst on the skateboard. A simple push would propel him down the ramp, over the jump and, if his calculations were correct, out into the hall and down the stairs before he landed in the couch cushions he had placed at the bottom of the stairs. Unfortunately for Timmy, he wasn't very good at math and his calculations were rarely correct. As he pushed off the top bunk, Timmy was on a crash course for his bedroom closet.

Timmy wasn't going fifty miles an hour when he hit the bike jump. But he was going fast enough to send him sailing four feet into the air, through his closet doors, and headfirst right through the back wall of his closet.

"What the . . ." he said.

Timmy didn't move. His head was completely embedded in the wall. After several seconds he let out a little cough and shook the dust from his hair. One minute he was traveling headfirst down the ramp, well on his way to becoming the world's greatest stuntman, and the next—the next minute he was launched headfirst into the wall, or a secret room behind it.

Timmy had set out to discover what it must have felt like to be Evel Knievel, flying high over the Snake River Canyon, but instead he had discovered Vincent Shadow's secret attic invention laboratory.

2

Minneapolis, Minnesota

Vincent Shadow used two rolls of duct

tape to connect nine garden hoses that he had borrowed from his neighbors. The garden hoses stretched from the kitchen through the living room, up the stairs, in and out of his stepsisters' bedrooms, into the bathroom (where they it ran in and out of a bathtub full of ice), and all the way back downstairs to the kitchen. A two-hundred-foot journey in all. A journey made possible by the generosity of Vincent Shadow's new neighbors.

As much as Vincent hated all the attention he had received for winning the annual Whizzer Toys invention contest, it had definitely made building his inventions easier. When he went door-to-door asking to borrow his neighbors' garden hoses, they were all eager to help the now-famous young inventor.

"Whatcha working on now, Vincent? A water hose that plays music? I betcha got a lot of ideas in that head of yours, dontcha," Mr. Johnston said.

"Ah, yeah. I guess so," Vincent replied.

But the truth was that Vincent had nothing. He hadn't had an idea hit him since he and his family moved to Minnesota five months ago. And to make matters worse, summer vacation was just two weeks away, which meant that his summer internship at Whizzer Toys was just two weeks away. Vincent would be spending his summer with the great toy inventor Howard G. Whiz himself. Howard was sure to expect inventions like Vincent's windless kite or his winning Pop Tunz sound bubbles. But, in a fit of frustration with all of his mishaps, Vincent had left all his inventions and notebooks in his secret attic lab back in New York. Now he had nothing. No notebooks. No new toys. No blinding inspiration. Nothing.

In an attempt to remedy this situation, Vincent purchased a shiny new black Moleskine notebook shortly after moving to Minnesota. He sat down and tried to fill it with all the inventions he could remember. But he only remembered a dozen or so. And most of them didn't work. Sky Writerz was one of those inventions. And now he was desperate to make it work.

Sky Writerz was a toy that would allow people to draw or write in midair with colored fog. Or at least Vincent had hoped it would. He had built several prototypes back in New York, but he was never able to make them work. The fog always drifted upward and the art ended up looking like something his mom would have liked: a Jackson Pollock painting, albeit a floating Jackson Pollock painting. But watching his breath hang in the cold Minnesota air had given him an idea. Maybe if he cooled the fog it would remain dense and hang in the air, like his breath on cold Minnesota mornings.

He dumped a gallon of water and two bottles of his sister's hand lotion into the fog machine. He needed glycerin to make fog and the label on his sister's fancy lotion claimed it was ninety-nine percent pure glycerin. Vincent lowered his safety goggles over his eyes and pushed the on button. The fog machine sat quietly. Then

it hissed and a small amount of smoke escaped from the duct-taped hoses. It smelled like lilacs, but Vincent didn't notice. He was too excited about the possibility of being the first person to create art in midair. Not even Picasso could make that claim.

Just then the hose began to shake violently. Vincent heard a loud crash upstairs. He set the end of the hose down and ran up the stairs to investigate. He had experienced dozens of mishaps in his old lab: cuts, scrapes, and explosions were just part of the job. In fact, it was the rare experiment that didn't have some sort of mishap. So Vincent was prepared for the worst when he walked into the bathroom. But he found nothing. The hose was still coiled under several pounds of ice. He checked all three of his stepsisters' bedrooms. Nothing. Nothing had exploded, imploded, or combusted.

"I must be getting—"

"VINCENT SHADOW!"

Vincent's self-congratulatory thoughts were interrupted by his stepsister Stella's scream.

"VINCENT, WHERE ARE YOU? WHAT'S GOING ON?" Stella yelled.

Vincent ran out of a bedroom and into a thick blanket of fog. He couldn't see a thing.

"I'm upstairs," he yelled.

"What's going on?" Stella demanded.

"Ah, looks like another failed experiment. Unfortunately," Vincent said, sounding defeated.

"You'd better get down here and get rid of this—this colored fog. Mom is gonna be home any minute.

And"—Stella waved her hand in front of her face—"what is that? It smells like—VINCENT SHADOW, DID YOU USE MY NEW LOTION?"

"All in the name of science, Sis. All in the name of science."

Vincent sat down and decided to wait for the fog, and his sister, to settle down.